"You've got me all figured out?"

If only he could figure her out. He'd love to know what she liked, disliked and find ways to make her smile. The thought was too big and stirred up a feeling he didn't want to dive into and swim around with.

"No, I don't. But what I have figured out is how to make things work out for the best. Win-win."

Tyrone watched her consider his words. He tried to appear calm despite the racing of his heart. If she said no then not only would he have to admit that he'd lied, but the admission would more than likely cost them the show. He needed her and he wasn't against begging if he had to.

"You really think this is going to work." She sounded doubtful, but there was a spark of interest in her eyes.

"Come on, Kiera, I know you know a good arrangement when it comes up. Look at how far the network went to make the wedding a hit. They hired seat fillers. You know they'll play up our love story and we'll both come out on top in the end. What do you say?"

He tipped his glass toward her. "Will you be my fake girlfriend?"

Dear Reader,

It is time for Tyrone Livingston to get his happily-ever-after! Tyrone is the baby brother, the hothead and the one who most wanted to take the ghost investigations from side hustle to a television show. He's finally achieved his dream, but Tyrone's impulsive nature is also threatening everything he and his brothers have achieved.

When a spontaneous kiss at a wedding brings his playboy past in the limelight and threatens his dream, he's willing to do anything to save the show. Kiera is attracted to Tyrone, but she also knows he's not the settle-down type. Fake dating Tyrone helps her career as a makeup artist, but can she really pretend and not fall for Tyrone?

I had so much fun writing not just this story but the entire series. You readers have really embraced the Livingston Brothers and shown them lots of love. Thank you so much for going on this amazing ride with me!

Happy reading,

Synithia

Counterfeit Courtship

SYNITHIA WILLIAMS

HARLEQUIN

SPECIAL
EDITION

Recycling programs
for this product may
not exist in your area.

ISBN-13: 978-1-335-72436-6

Counterfeit Courtship

Copyright © 2022 by Synithia R. Williams

Harlequin Enterprises ULC
22 Adelaide St. West, 41st Floor
Toronto, Ontario M5H 4E3, Canada
www.Harlequin.com

Printed in U.S.A.

Synithia Williams has been an avid romance-novel lover since picking up her first at the age of thirteen. It was only natural that she would begin penning her own romances soon after—much to the chagrin of her high school math teachers. She's a native of South Carolina and now writes romances as hot as their Southern settings. Outside of writing, she works on water quality and sustainability issues for local government. She's married to her own personal hero, and they have two sons, who have convinced her that professional wrestling and superheroes are supreme entertainment. When she isn't working, writing or being a wife and mother, she's usually bingeing a TV series, playing around on social media or planning her next girls' night out with friends. You can learn more about Synithia by visiting her website, www.synithiawilliams.com.

Books by Synithia Williams

Harlequin Special Edition

Heart & Souls

Summoning Up Love
The Spirit of Second Chances

HQN

Jackson Falls

The Promise of a Kiss
Forbidden Promises
Scandalous Secrets
Careless Whispers
Foolish Hearts

Visit the Author Profile page
at Harlequin.com for more titles.

To everyone making a way to live their dream.

Chapter One

Tyrone Livingston followed the short female usher who was dressed in a strapless peach dress down the aisle. White folding chairs flanked them to the left and right while the sweet scent of the huge yellow-and-purple flower bouquets filled the ballroom. The large-paned windows overlooking midtown Atlanta provided the perfect breathtaking backdrop for a romantic wedding.

"You can sit here," the usher said with a small smile as she indicated a seat on the left side.

Tyrone glanced down the row filled nearly to capacity except for the two chairs on the end, then back at rows of empty seats behind. He wasn't against sitting next to strangers, but when there were plenty of open seats, he'd prefer elbow room over cramming in.

"Do you mind if I sit back there?" He pointed to the empty seats several rows behind.

The usher's smile didn't waver as she shook her head. "I do. We're filling up the front seats then moving toward the back. It's better for pictures."

He eyed the extra space, then the usher, whose expression dared him to make a scene at this wedding. Tyrone's irritation flared, but he was not going to make a scene. The entire point of attending this wedding was to make a good impression with the network that hosted the ghost-investigation show he had with his brothers. Arguing with an usher about a seat wasn't worth potentially pissing off someone before the wedding even started.

"No problem," he said. He sat in the empty chair at the end of the aisle. The usher tapped his shoulder. "Please slide down one for the next guest."

Tyrone blinked. If he wasn't going to have elbow room, he'd at least prefer the leg room he could get from the aisle seat, but again, the usher stared as if she was waiting for a reason to escort him out. He held up a hand and nodded before sliding over.

The man to his left, a guy who was tall and built like a professional wrestler, shifted in his seat when Tyrone's shoulder bumped his. "My bad, man," Tyrone said.

"We cool," the guy replied and tried to put a few centimeters between his arm and Tyrone's.

If they both held themselves at stiff, awkward

angles maybe they'd avoid rubbing against each other for the entire ceremony. Tyrone scanned the crowd of people for anyone he recognized. When the executives at the Exploration Channel invited him and his brothers to the wedding of Sofia Gomez and Tanner Logan, two of the network's most popular stars, Tyrone had immediately agreed. Their ghost-investigation show, *Haunted Homeboys*, had premiered the previous season. They'd gotten good reviews and generated some buzz online and with the media, but they had a long way to go before becoming a household name. The network had just started discussions with them about a second season, which was why Tyrone spent every moment he could trying to connect with others at the network and build interest in their show.

A few hosts of other shows were interspersed in the crowd. Most of the people, like the guy next to him, he didn't recognize. That didn't mean much. Sofia and Tanner were celebrities. Their family cooking show was one of the channel's highest-rated shows, which meant they probably had a wide circle of friends.

The usher was back down the aisle, this time with a woman behind her. She pointed to the empty seat next to Tyrone. "You can sit here."

Tyrone glanced up and met a pair of alluring dark eyes. He sat up straighter. Not just alluring eyes, but thick, kissable lips, smooth, pecan-brown skin, a short sexy haircut and a delectable figure encased in a capped-sleeve, soft yellow dress that dared any-one in the room to ignore the curvy hips and full breasts within.

Her head tilted to the side as she watched him. His mouth was open. He snapped it shut and jerked his eyes forward. He was here to mingle and network. Not drool over the curvy queen sitting next to him.

"Thank you," she said to the usher in a low, husky voice before sitting.

Her arm brushed against his. She glanced at him quickly. "Excuse me." She shifted to give him space.

Tyrone also shifted away. He didn't like the way the shock of her brief touch reverberated throughout his body. He knew what it meant when a woman's touch lingered in his memory. It meant he was at-tracted. Instincts made him want to follow the attrac-tion. To chat, flirt, turn on the charm and ultimately, hopefully, end up with the woman in his arms.

He was holding back on his instincts right now. Rumors of him being some type of playboy had sur-faced just as the show had premiered. He didn't con-sider himself a playboy, but since he did enjoy the company of women and wasn't in the market for anything other than casual dating the word *play-boy* was frequently thrown around. The good peo-ple at the Exploration Network worried the rumors would harm the brothers' images and ultimately the show's ratings.

He could be good and suppress his instincts for one

day. Well, several days. However many days it took to convince the network to sign them for a second season.

His elbow bumped the guy to his left. He gave the man another apologetic look. "These seats are packed tight, huh."

The man nodded before turning to the person next to him. Curvy Queen moved in her chair and brushed against him again. He glanced her way and she sighed.

"They really could've put more room between these chairs," she said under her breath.

"I wonder why they didn't," Tyrone replied, even though she hadn't spoken directly to him.

Dark eyes, deep and rich like chocolate, met his. "They're trying to fit a lot of people in a tight space. You know, anything for appearances," she said with a raised eyebrow and a half smile, but there was no malice in her voice.

More people were led in and packed into the rows behind them. "How many people are they trying to fit in here?"

"I heard they wanted a three-hundred-person wedding," Queen answered.

Tyrone's eyes widened. "Three hundred people? Why would they try and fit three hundred people in here?"

"Again, appearances," she said, as if that was normal.

Maybe it was, but as the thigh of the man next to

him pressed into Tyrone's, he knew he wasn't a fan of three-hundred-person weddings for appearances. He shifted closer to the woman and tried to leave enough space so he wouldn't touch her. That was almost worse. Feeling the heat of her body next to his only made him hyperaware. As if an electric current pulsed next to him with each beat of his heart.

He needed to focus on something other than her nearness. "So, are you a friend of the bride or groom?" he asked in a rush.

She pursed her full lips, painted a dark berry color, as if considering. "Hmm…both, I guess. You?"

He shrugged. "Neither really. I've got a new show on their network and was invited."

He'd intentionally dropped the news about the show. He wanted to see the spark of interest in her eye. Wanted her to ask what show, so he could tell her about his work investigating ghosts. Then watch her interest grow before he flipped things to ask about her. He most definitely wanted to know more about her.

She nodded slowly. "Ahh." She leaned in and whispered. "So you're a seat filler, too."

Tyrone blinked and frowned. "A what? A seat filler?" he said, as if the words would make more sense the second time around.

He didn't know what she was talking about. "Nah, the network invited me because they want me to get to know the other stars."

She looked at him as if waiting for him to say he

was joking. "The network is trying to fill seats for Sofia and Tanner's wedding," she said with a this-is-obvious smile.

"They wouldn't have a problem filling the seats. They're two of the network's biggest stars."

She raised an eyebrow and looked as if she was going to contradict him, then shook her head. "Maybe, but I know they hired me to fill a seat because they didn't have enough people to show up."

Tyrone frowned and glanced around at the growing crowd, then turned to the guy next to him. "Excuse me, but are you a friend of the bride or groom?"

The guy had a moment of hesitation before giving a nonchalant shrug. "Uhh…groom."

"How do you know him?"

"I work at the gym where he works out. He invited me and a few other trainers."

Tyrone nodded before turning back to the woman. She had a smirk that told him she'd heard the entire conversation. "He's a seat filler, too?" Tyrone whispered under his breath.

The Queen laughed a husky laugh he felt all the way across his body and down to his toes. She winked. "Told ya."

Tyrone sat back in the chair and took in the fancy decor, packed seats and strategically placed cameras all over the room. "Well, I'll be damned."

Chapter Two

"Okay, Queen, what do you think? Seat filler or true guest?"

Kiera Cox smirked at Tyrone standing next to her by the bar. He knew her name now, but continued to refer to her as "Queen." She liked that. Probably more than she should have.

Tyrone was obviously a flirt and a ladies' man, but she wasn't turned off by flirty men. If anything, she was drawn to them…unfortunately. The attentive ones typically knew how to make a woman feel good in and out of the bedroom. But, while she enjoyed the attention, being drawn to men like him meant she also knew his interest was superficial—something she wasn't in the market for ever again.

Tyrone raised his eyebrows and tilted his head to

the side. Kiera turned and considered the woman he'd indicated. She immediately shook her head. "Seat filler. I know her from another wedding."

Tyrone's eyes widened. They were brown and changed to the color of whiskey, depending on the lighting. Hypnotic eyes she was sure he used to his advantage. "Another wedding? Do you do this every weekend?"

He sounded surprised and intrigued by the possibility. Kiera chuckled and sipped the glass of champagne in her hand. Tyrone was also very cute. Cocoa-brown skin, deep-set bedroom eyes, a clean-cut moustache and goatee, and stylish a fade. He was tall, but she didn't think he topped six feet, and the dark green fitted suit he was wearing drew her attention to the nice body it covered.

She raised a shoulder. "I've filled in for a few other weddings."

He leaned in closer. His cologne drifted toward her, a smooth, citrusy scent that made her mouth water. "Other celebrities?"

"Not just celebrities. Businesspeople, online influencers, you name it. Pretty much anyone who wants to make a good impression or wants the world to believe a ton of people can't wait to celebrate their happy occasion."

"Wow… I never would have thought of that. Is this what you do for a living? Attend weddings?"

She shook her head. "It's what I do on the side for

fun and extra money, because I love going to weddings."

"For the romance?"

She wiggled the champagne flute in her hand. "For the open bar, the meal, cake and dancing. It's better than going to the club."

He laughed and shook his head. "You joking?"

Kiera shook her head and leaned one elbow on the high-top table they occupied. "No, I'm not. If a couple is willing to pay for a seat filler like me, then they're willing to go all out for their wedding. The bar is always open. The food is always on point. I have yet to meet a flavor of cake I didn't enjoy, and I will Cupid-Shuffle and Electric-Slide the hell out of anyone in here."

Tyrone's shoulders shook as he laughed harder. He was even cuter when he laughed. She wasn't here to pick up a guy. Her reasons for coming included more than her love of weddings. She needed money and connections. Connections to help her fledgling business as a makeup artist successful and the money that would come with the high-end clientele in and around Atlanta. So, while she was single after breaking things off with Mike, her long-term, on-again, off-again, kind-of boyfriend, she couldn't really afford to have a one-night stand with Tyrone Livingston, could she?

Nope! You're trying to work on his show. This is not how we do things, Kiera!

Kiera pulled her focus away from Tyrone's sexy smile and focused on the conversation. "Wait until after they throw the bouquet and cut the cake. I'll show you how I get down on the dance floor."

"Alright, I look forward to that." His laughter faded and he looked at her with renewed interest and just the right amount of desire. "So, what else do you do besides fill seats at weddings?"

She flipped her wrist then framed the side of her face with her hand. "Ta-da." When his eyebrows drew together, she grinned. "My beautiful face. I'm a makeup artist."

"Ah, okay. That's cool."

"I know. I love it and that's the other reason why I do this. I've been lucky enough to do the makeup of a few of the people at the Exploration Network, but that's it. I'm hoping that I'll be able to work it out to be the lead makeup artist on one of their shows."

Kiera watched for his reaction. Sometimes people, her immediate family mostly, viewed her love of makeup and interest in becoming a makeup artist as "not a real job." They didn't understand why she'd major in business only to turn around and "play in makeup" as her grandmother once said. Her mom and dad tried to be supportive, but they still believed makeup was just something to put on for special occasions versus a way to make money. If Tyrone gave any hint of being one of the people who chose to tease her about her "little makeup job" then she would walk away immediately.

"Nice," he said, nodding his head. "What got you into makeup?"

She let out a breath and relaxed. Score another point for Tyrone. "I've always been interested. I partially blame my mom. She refused to let me wear makeup in middle school because I had terrible acne. I wanted to wear it to cover up said acne. She insisted that makeup would make it worse."

"Does it?"

"Some products can, and if you're not taking care of your skin you can make the problem worse. I didn't know that in middle school. I snuck around to put on makeup. Unfortunately, with my preteen salary of exactly whatever money I could finagle out of my dad, I couldn't afford quality products. Everything I used did make things worse."

He cringed. "Yikes."

She sipped her champagne and shrugged. "Pretty much. Of course, my mom said, 'I told you so' and I lost the war on makeup."

"But not forever, I assume, considering your job."

"You're correct. I was so determined to live my glamorous and fabulous life as a makeup artist that I went to cosmetology school after college. I learned more about products and skin care so I could make my clients feel beautiful whether they're wearing makeup or not."

She skipped over the long, sad years between middle school and college, when she had to deal with the taunts and teasing of classmates about her "bumpy" face, or how they could draw various pictures connecting the dots from the acne scars. And the mound of debt she'd incurred moving out of her parents' home in east Atlanta to attend the fancy cosmetology school in Buckhead and live in an equally fancy apartment to match her dreams of "adult life." Those were hurts and secrets not worth sharing with a cute guy who may or may not become her one-night stand.

Tyrone softly clapped and gave an appreciative nod. "You learned both the makeup and the skin care. Go ahead, Queen."

Heat filled her cheeks. His praise shouldn't make her blush. He was only flirting, but damn if flirting with him didn't feel good.

Remember why you're here.

"Who does the makeup on your show?" She already knew the answer. Eliza Cole had been the previous makeup artist on his ghost-investigation show. Just like she'd pretended she didn't recognize him the moment the usher asked her to sit beside him, she played it cool now. The trick to getting what she wanted was to not show just how bad she wanted it.

"Her name was Eliza. She was cool and she worked with a few people. I heard she's moving on to their show." He pointed to the bride and groom.

That's exactly what Kiera had heard. Eliza had worked as the lead makeup artist on a few Exploration shows and all her hard work paid off. She was now the lead on several of the larger, more popular shows, leaving a position wide open and perfect for Kiera.

"Maybe I can get on your show," Kiera said, as if the idea just came to her. "I've put my name in the hat to replace Eliza on a few series."

"I think I'd like that."

His immediate answer was encouraging. She didn't know what she'd expected. It wasn't as if a man flirting with her would shoot down her dream. She hadn't expected such a quick and eager reply.

"Why is that?"

"Why do you think?" He leaned in close enough for the heat of his body to brush against hers and lowered his voice. "Because I'd get to see more of you." He didn't remain in her space, but leaned back. She had the strongest urge to follow his movement and ease closer to him.

"How much more of me do you want to see?" she asked with a half smile over her glass of champagne. Keeping her voice light and hiding the excited pounding of her heart with an amused tone took a colossal act of strength.

"A whole lot more."

A shiver of anticipation danced across her skin. Tyrone Livingston was the kind of guy she promised herself to avoid, and the kind that always had her breaking her own rules. If he kept on talking like that, then he just might end up seeing a lot more of her.

Chapter Three

Tyrone couldn't keep his eyes off Kiera dancing next to him. Her head thrown back as she laughed, hips swaying to the music and skin glowing thanks to the sheen of sweat she'd worked up dancing. All of those things combined to make her mesmerizing.

She'd been right. The wedding had turned out to be a lot more fun than he'd expected. The bar was indeed open, the food delicious, and he'd enjoyed watching her dodge the bouquet when it was thrown so she could finish her slice of cake. Not only that, but she also knew people. Not just the seat fillers in attendance, but several people from the Exploration Network, along with the other celebrities and influencers in attendance. She'd researched who they were and where they worked, and casually dropped a line about her skills with a makeup brush and her willingness to work in most conversations.

He was impressed. And turned on. A dangerous combination.

The upbeat music ended, and the band slowed things down. Tyrone turned to Kiera and opened his arms, more than willing to feel her body against his. Kiera shook her head and waved a hand in front of her face.

"I'm hot and need some water."

Pushing aside his disappointment, he smiled. Maybe there'd be plenty of time later to have her in his arms. "Come on, let's go to the bar and get something to cool you off."

He placed a hand on the small of her back and led her off the dance floor toward the bar. Her body was warm and soft beneath his palm. He fought the urge to trace the line of her curves that vibrated through him with every brush of her dress against his palm.

Once they were seated at the bar and Kiera had a glass of ice water, he spoke. "You meant it when you said you were going to tear up the dance floor."

She'd just taken a sip of water and put a hand in front of her mouth to stifle her laugh. After she swallowed, she nodded. "Did you think I was lying?"

"Not at all, but I still enjoyed watching you have fun."

Her dark brown eyes sparkled beneath the lights in the ballroom as she watched him. "I think you had fun, too. You were just as enthusiastic as I was out on that dance floor."

"You're right."

"So, you love to dance, too?" She sipped her water and ran her tongue over her lower lip.

Tyrone's stomach clenched and he inched closer. The woman was like a magnet, and he was iron, helpless against her pull. "I won't say I love it, but I'm not against dancing and having a good time. I used to host promotional parties and other events for the radio station I worked with back home. I couldn't go to a party and not dance. Getting the crowd hyped was part of what I had to do for the job."

She held up a finger. "Wait a second. You were a hype man before you started this show?"

Tyrone chuckled at the surprise in her voice. "Not quite a hype man. I worked promotions and sales for a station out of Myrtle Beach, South Carolina. Part of promotions was taking care of the after parties the radio station had whenever there was a concert in the area and the singer would typically also come by the station for an interview with one of the DJs. I'd help coordinate the visit between their publicist and the station."

"Impressive," she said with a raised eyebrow.

He'd loved that job. All he'd wanted when he was younger was to get out of Sunshine Beach, the small town he'd grown up in on the coast of South Carolina. He'd dreamed of living a life of fun and excitement, but had stuck around because he hadn't wanted to abandon his brothers. Not after his oldest brother, Dion, gave up college to take care of Tyrone and their middle brother, Wesley, after their parents died. Working at the radio station, planning parties and meeting celebrities, was the next best thing until they'd gotten the show.

"It was fun. I got to do a lot of fun things and meet new people. It's how I ended up with the show. I met our producer, Tiana, when she was in town for a party the station hosted. I told her about my side hustle with my brothers investigating ghosts and she mentioned they were starting a paranormal investigation lineup. The rest—" He waved a hand.

"As they say, is history," she said, finishing for him. "Well, now that you have the show, is it everything you hoped it would be?"

"It's everything and more. I just don't want to screw things up."

"How would you screw things up?"

Considering how he would like to see her again, he decided to not mention the rumors about him and his not-so-stellar dating history. He wasn't ashamed of his past; he was always upfront and honest in every relationship about not being ready to settle down or wanting anything too serious. That didn't mean he wanted to see disappointment or, worse, rejection in her eyes if he brought up his past. He didn't want her to see him as a screwup, the way so many people had and sometimes still did. He wanted to see where the night would lead. He wasn't a romantic person who expected the night, and this feeling, to lead to anything life-changing, but that didn't mean he didn't want to enjoy whatever time he could get with her.

"The network is waiting to see how the first season does before agreeing to sign for a second," he said. "I'm worried about everything, including how well the first season goes. I want them to renew the show."

"I've seen the first season. I don't think you'll have to worry about being renewed. You and your brothers have great on-screen chemistry, and you're perfect at what you do. If they don't sign on for a second season, then their loss."

His eyes widened. "Oh, so you've seen my show."

She glanced away quickly and grinned. "I mean… I keep up with the network."

He reached over and brushed his fingers across her forearm. "So, you knew who I was when you sat down next to me?"

Her breathing hitched and flirtation sparked in her eyes. "Not immediately, but yeah, after we got to talking, I realized who you were."

The typical excitement of knowing someone recognized him waned. Knowing who he was could also mean she'd heard the rumors. "What have you heard…about the show, I mean?"

She took another sip of her water. "Good things so

far. That's why I don't think you have to worry about the network. They're going to bring you all back. From what I've heard, they're always way late with signing on for the next year."

He relaxed and glanced around the ballroom. She hadn't heard any bad rumors about him. The party was still in full swing, but most of the wedding activities were done. He focused on her. "What are you doing when you leave here?"

She slowly lowered her cup back to the bar. One corner of her pouty lips lifted in a slight smile that sent his heart into overdrive. "That depends."

"On what?"

"On what's good to get into after this is all over." The sparkle in her eye turned his blood into flames.

Oh, he had a lot of good ideas of what she could get into when this was over. Ideas involving her curves entered his mind, their mouths connecting in a passionate kiss, legs and arms entangled in an intimate embrace. "I've got a few ideas…" His voice had gone husky with the desire pulsing through his veins.

"Do you?" She sipped her water and the tip of her tongue traced across her lower lip.

Desire punched through his midsection. "Most definitely."

"What are your ideas?"

He slid closer and pulled a piece of lint out of her hair. The strands were soft and silky against his fingers, making him want to slide his fingers through the sleek tresses, cup the back of her head and lower his mouth to hers. "You and me, someplace quiet." He dropped his hand and let his fingers trail across her shoulder and arm.

Her body shivered slightly before she smiled. "I kind of like the sound of that."

Kiera did like the sound of Tyrone's offer. She'd love to follow him up to one of the ridiculously expensive rooms in the hotel that was hosting this wedding, undress and discover if he could back up the promise in his eyes, with crumpled sheets, cries of pleasure and bone-melting satisfaction. But she couldn't find out if he could live up to it or not. What she'd love more would be to get the job as lead makeup artist for his show.

Spending time with him tonight had shown her that she liked Tyrone on top of being attracted to him. He was fun, funny and full of life. They got along, and if they became lovers, the time together would be fun…while it lasted. If they became lovers *and* coworkers, once the love affair ended things could quickly become tricky and awkward.

She finished her water, then met his eyes. "But, as fun as that sounds, I really should be getting home."

His frown was cute. "You're leaving me?"

Kiera grinned then reached out and patted his cheek. "Not leaving you. Just going home to rest."

His fingers circled her wrist before she could pull back. He didn't hold her tight. If she wanted to break the hold, she could easily do it. His eyes were playful as they met hers. "It feels a lot like leaving." His thumb brushed across the sensitive skin inside her wrist.

Tingles from the touch traipsed across her arms, neck and chest, tightening her nipples as a heat wave spread through her body. Damn, he was good at temptation. "I'm hoping I'll see you again."

"Oh, really?"

"Yep, when they hire me on as the makeup artist for your show. Then we'll be coworkers."

He nodded and grinned, then a heartbeat later understanding dawned, and his grin diminished. "Coworkers." He let go of her wrist and leaned back.

"Mmm-hmm. Now do you understand why it's best for me to go?"

"I understand, and even though a part of me is screaming we're not coworkers yet..." He glanced down. Kiera's eyes followed his to the bulge between his legs. She felt good knowing the simple touch and flirtation had affected him just as much as her. He raised his gaze back to hers. "I am smart enough to listen to this head most of the time." He tapped his temple.

Kiera laughed, once again charmed by his humor. "A man who knows how to listen to his brain over his libido. You just might be a saint."

He grunted. "Far from a saint. Can I walk you out, at least?"

"I'd be disappointed if you didn't."

She slid off the barstool. Tyrone put his hand on the small of her back as they left the ballroom. She liked his touch and wanted to lean in closer. When his hand shifted from her back to her hip, she realized she had leaned in, and he'd taken the opportunity to pull her against his side. Even though she knew she should step out of his embrace, she enjoyed the heat of his body, strong and stable, next to hers. For the minute or so it would take to leave the hotel she could treat herself to a small pleasure of being held in his arms. There was absolutely nothing wrong with a little indulgence.

Once outside of the ballroom, Kiera headed toward the lobby, but Tyrone's hand around her waist pulled her in the opposite direction. Her eyes widened, and she followed along as he swept her behind one of the tall plants against the wall.

He held her close, but again loose enough that if she wanted to break away, she could. His eyes were intense as they stared into hers. "If I'm out of line, let me know and I'll let you go," he said in a low, sensual voice. "But I really don't want to send you home without at least kissing you."

Her heart slammed against her rib cage as if she was still on the dance floor. Her breath stuck in her throat and the heat wave from before became an all-consuming inferno. "What about me working with you?"

"If you get the job, we'll pretend this never happened and work together like responsible adults."

A load of crap if she'd ever heard it. The passion in his eyes and the way her pulse pounded meant that the only way she'd be able to forget this kiss is if it was one of the worst kisses she'd ever experienced. Her eyes lowered to his plump lower lip. This would not be a terrible kiss.

"Am I out of line?" His hand drifted away from her hip.

Kiera grabbed the front of his suit jacket and hauled him forward. She pressed her mouth against his and slid her tongue across his full lower lip. Tyrone stood stunned for a second, but within a breath, one hand cupped the back of her head and the other snaked around her waist. He pressed her body flush against his. Solid chest to full breasts, abs to stomach and the enchanting poke of his erection against her soft heat. Not only did his body feel amazing, but he also kissed so damn good. His lips and tongue glided and played across her own in a dance that made her sigh and push against him.

He followed her lead, or maybe just took over completely, because in an instant her back was against the wall. His knee nudged between hers' and Kiera opened so he could fit between her legs.

He pulled back slowly. "I need to stop?" The words

were more of a question and he gave her a pleading look.

This was her chance to throw caution to the wind and be spontaneous. She really wanted to be spontaneous. Her bank account and the mountain of debt she needed to pay off screamed louder. She needed to work at the Exploration Network. She needed the money from a lucrative career more than she needed Tyrone to give her an orgasm.

She nodded. "Yes."

He lifted and lowered his chin before stepping back. They didn't touch and walked in silence to the front of the hotel, where Kiera gave her ticket to valet for her car. The warm night air did little to cool the fire of desire raging in her veins. The heat and humidity coated her, made her want to slip naked between cool sheets with Tyrone next to her.

"Can I at least have your number in case...?" he said.

"In case I don't get the job?" she asked with a raised eyebrow.

"Nah, I hope you get the job. I had fun tonight. Call me. Let me know how things go?" He held out his phone. "Put in your number."

Kiera took his phone and entered her number. There was a spark there. Even though she hoped networking tonight would land her the job doing makeup for his show, she could end up doing the makeup for someone else. If that was the case, then she'd have no reason to not follow up.

Except he's a playboy and you don't mess with players anymore!

She ignored the vow she'd made after breaking things off with Mike. That was her problem. She always ignored promises she made to protect her heart. She was a sucker for sex appeal and a winning personality. Maybe in the light of day she'd realize that, regardless of where she landed, hooking up with a guy like Tyrone was not smart.

She handed back his phone as the attendant pulled up with her car. "Until next time, Tyrone." Since it wasn't the light of day, and her body was still hot and sticky with desire, she lifted on her toes and gave him one last quick kiss before getting into her car and getting the hell out of there.

Chapter Four

Tyrone flicked on the lamp behind his laptop before changing the setting from bright to a more muted light. With the curtains open in his hotel room in midtown Atlanta and the lamp turned on, the room was bright enough that he didn't look as if he was sitting in the back of a cave. He opened the calendar on his laptop and navigated to the link to the virtual-meeting platform. As he waited to be connected, he checked his image in the camera. He nodded with satisfaction at the lighting and the angle just as notification popped up that the meeting was starting.

Three boxes filled his laptop screen, two showing each of his brothers and the third with him. His oldest brother, Dion, sat in his office, where he worked as the public-works director for a small town outside of Charlotte, North Carolina. A light blue polo shirt stretched across his wide shoulders, and he ran a hand over his bald head. His middle brother, Wesley, sat at his kitchen table in front of the closed blinds of the sliding glass door that led to his condo's backyard. He wore a short-sleeved dark button-up shirt and his short, curly hair needed a cut. A fourth screen popped up and their agent, Lauren, joined the call. A white woman in her late forties, with sleek dark brown hair, square-framed glasses and a straightforward personality, Lauren was in a leather chair in her home office. The wall behind her was filled with various plaques and awards of her different clients.

Tyrone smiled when he saw his brothers on screen. They hadn't hung out in several weeks. With Dion in North Carolina, Wesley still in Sunshine Beach and Tyrone spending most of his time in Atlanta, they didn't spend as much time together. Once upon a time, he would have loved to have so much separation from his brothers. Now that he had it, he missed the days when they lived together.

"Dion, why are you still at work?" Tyrone asked. Both of his brothers had kept their day jobs and made a way to make it work between filming. Tyrone had spent the time after filming attending network events and trying to drum up interest in the show. It was 7:00 p.m. on a Friday. Dion, despite being the most dedicated person he knew, shouldn't have been in his office.

Dion shook his head. "There was a storm yesterday and we've just had a press conference with updates on cleanup."

"You've got to do the press conference?" Wesley asked.

Dion rubbed his eyes and shook his head. "Nah, but I do have to be there in case there are any questions."

Lauren nodded and leaned toward the camera. "Then I won't keep you three long. I just want to give you all an update on the call I had with the network executives earlier today."

Excitement jumped in Tyrone's chest. "Are they ready to talk about doing a second season?"

Lauren held up a hand. "The first season is going very well. Your show was well received and now that the three of you are interacting with the fans on social media during the replay of season one, that's generated even more buzz. People are loving watching the three of you work together to investigate ghosts and help people."

Tyrone nodded and grinned at the screen. Wesley and Dion did the same. That was good news and exactly what they needed to hear. If they could build a cult following, then that would go a long way toward proving their show was worth renewing.

"That's great," Tyrone said. "That's what we wanted, right? What did the executives say?"

"They're happy about the reaction to the show," Lauren said. "But…"

Unease bubbled in Tyrone's stomach. "But what?"

Lauren sighed and clicked a few keys on the keyboard. "But that was until this showed up online this afternoon."

The screen flickered, and the squares with their faces shrunk while a picture of Tyrone kissing a woman pressed against a wall filled most of the screen. His heart dropped to his feet. Tension blossomed behind his left eye. He rubbed his temple while his brothers both spoke up.

"What the hell is that?" Wesley asked.

"Seriously, Tyrone," Dion said in the disappointed "dad" voice that always made Tyrone's neck tighten.

"Where did you get that?" Tyrone asked instead of addressing his brothers' outbursts.

Lauren sighed before speaking. "It's online. Someone posted it and tagged the network and your show's social-media accounts. The poster is once again claiming that you're a womanizer and a player and is using this as proof."

"Who is that?" Dion asked. "Do you even know her name?"

Tyrone clenched his teeth. He was not about to get into an argument with his older brother. He knew that regardless of the answer, Dion was disappointed in him again. That was nothing new. He squinted at the screen and immediately recognized the woman in the yellow dress. He would recognize her anywhere. Hell, he hadn't been able to get the memory of that moment out of his head in the weeks since, and he'd tried.

"Her name is Kiera," he said.

Even though the screen was small, Dion's smirk and eye roll was clearly visible. "Kiera who?"

Tyrone couldn't remember her last name. Damn, how could he have forgotten her last name? "She's a makeup artist. She also does makeup for some of the stars at the network."

"You mean Kiera Cox?" Lauren asked.

"You know her?" He wasn't going to agree to anything until he was sure Lauren wasn't trying to trip him up with the wrong last name. He had to figure out a way to fix this and his brain was still in shock.

Lauren nodded. "Yes, I met her at a wedding last fall. She did the makeup for the bride and the wedding party. She's worked as a makeup artist in Atlanta for a while. I think Eliza recommended her to take over at your show."

That was enough to convince him they were talking about the same Kiera. He crossed his fingers and hoped he wasn't about to make things worse. "That's her," Tyrone said.

"Okay, so now we know who she is," Dion said, cutting in. "Can you tell us why you were kissing her against the wall like that?"

"Yeah, Tyrone," Wes said. "I thought you were chilling with the women because of the rumors."

His brothers threw out questions faster than Tyrone could think. The tension behind his eyes grew with each word. "She's my girlfriend," Tyrone said, blurting out the only answer that would be acceptable in the face of the displeasure in his brothers' voices.

"Your girlfriend?" Wesley and Dion shouted at the same time.

"Yeah...my girlfriend. We met a few weeks ago here in Atlanta and went to the wedding together. I didn't think anything was wrong with kissing her after the wedding," He said everything in a rush. The way he always did when he'd messed up and needed to fix the problem. It was a habit he'd picked up in high school. He went with whatever came to mind that would get him in the least amount of trouble and was less likely to result in him and Dion getting into a fight. It had gotten him out of worse situations so far.

"Since when did you get a girlfriend?" Dion asked.

"I don't tell you all everything."

"Yes, you do," Wesley chimed in.

He scrambled for an excuse that his brothers would believe. "Well...we just agreed to be exclusive. I haven't had the time to tell anyone. I really like her. I wanted to make sure it was real before I said anything."

"Are you saying you two are really dating?" Lauren asked.

"We are."

Lauren slapped her hands together. "That's actually great! The network loves couples. The fans love seeing the small snippets of your regular life on the show. They'd mentioned having more behind-the-scenes sections in season two. The fans really want to see more of your day-to-day life. Maybe having your girlfriend on the show, working with you, along with the scenes of Dion and Vanessa and Wesley with Cierra will be a good idea."

"Huh?" Tyrone said, feeling as if he was about to tumble off a cliff. A cliff he'd rushed at full speed.

"Yes, I love this." Lauren got rid of the picture of Wesley and Kiera kissing. Their faces filled the screen. He coud see excitement on her face; suspicion clouded his brothers' expressions. "Let me call the network back and explain. This could work out to be just what we need to get your show renewed for another season."

Kiera put her finger over her mouth to shush her brother, Rodrick, in the middle of his update on the latest drama with his girlfriend, Contessa. They were on the couch in the living room of her apartment. She'd ordered nachos, her brother's favorite food, as she listened to the reason why Contessa was mad at him. Typically, Contessa was right to be mad. Her brother didn't cheat, but he also flirted when given the opportunity. He valued her opinion on women and in most cases she could get him to see the light, apologize and go back home to the one woman who put up with his foolishness.

Rodrick scowled but stopped in midsentence and leaned back on Kiera's red couch. Kiera couldn't believe he'd actually listened to her on the first try. Rodrick typically wasn't so accommodating, but maybe the surprise on her face when she'd seen the number on her phone was enough to shock him into silence.

Kiera sat up straight, cleared her throat and answered the call from her contact at the Exploration Network. "Hello," she said in her best, professional, hire-me-immediately voice.

Rodrick snickered and made a face. Kiera kicked him, hoping he'd hush, but he slapped her ankle in retaliation. She bit her lip to hold back a yelp and held up a hand as if to punch him. Rodrick just slid farther away from her on the couch.

"Kiera, hello, this is Tiana Hill. Did I catch you at a bad time?"

Kiera shook her head. "No. I'm working on my latest video, but I've come to a stopping point."

She had been working on her latest makeup tutorial before Rodrick showed up to figure out if he really wasn't doing enough to help Contessa around the house with their two-year-old son. When Kiera had started her online channel two years ago on skin care and makeup she hadn't expected much. It was right after she'd fallen, broken her foot and had too much time on her hands because she couldn't stand and do makeup. Beauty channels were a dime a dozen. Yet, somehow, people liked Kiera's approach and gravitated to her updates. The money she made wasn't enough to get her out of the debt from a health emergency and no insurance, but it did help her buy the quality products she used for clients.

"Oh, good. I can't wait to see it," Tiana said. "You know I love your makeup tutorials. You're building quite a following on YouTube."

Kiera grinned and was glad to know Tiana was aware of Kiera's growing following. Tiana had stumbled upon her channel and reached out to Kiera to do her makeup before a party. That's when she'd recommended Kiera to other people at the network if they needed a makeup artist.

"Thank you," Kiera said. "I'll be sure to give you a shout-out in this video."

She planned to get back to it when she finished her brother's counseling session. If she didn't know how much Rodrick and Contessa really loved each other and that they kind of thrived off the drama of their relationship, then she would tell them both to move on with their lives and be free.

"That would be cool." Tiana sounded excited, which was funny to Kiera. Tiana was a television producer. Her name appeared in the credits of legit shows—for her to be excited about being mentioned on Kiera's YouTube channel was funny and humbling. "I'll most definitely like and share if you do. But that's not why I called. I have some really great news."

"Well, lay it on me because I like getting really great news."

"We'd like to bring you on as the lead makeup artist for the *Haunted Homeboys* show!"

"You would?" Kiera grinned, reached over and slapped her brother's leg repeatedly. She managed to keep her voice moderately calm even though she wanted to shout for joy.

Rodrick kicked at her until she stopped hitting him. Kiera pressed her hand over her pounding heart.

"Yes. We think this would be a great angle for the direction of the show next season."

The word choice was odd, but that wasn't enough to dim her enthusiasm. "A great angle?"

"Yes! You may not know, but the network is really trying to focus on relationships and family on a lot of their shows next season. They want more behind-the-scenes action and insights into the real lives of our stars. It's a way to humanize them while also playing up the emotional connections with the viewers. This season they hope to find out which couples resonate with the viewers. Possibly for future spinoffs."

"Oh really…well, that's good." Kiera didn't see what that had to do with her.

"So, of course, the idea of having you and Tyrone Livingston working together on the same show would be a great way to play into this. Seriously, Kiera, why didn't you tell me you two were dating?"

Kiera coughed and sat up straight. "Huh?"

"Don't play with me. The picture of the two of you kissing is all over social media today. Didn't you see it?"

The blood drained from Kiera's face. There were pictures of them kissing? How in the world could there be pictures? They'd hid behind a bush. Wasn't a bush the universal perfect cover when you didn't want to be seen? "N-no, I didn't see it."

"Well, at first the network viewed this as a potential scandal. You know everyone says Tyrone is a player and there is a small group of people online who are going after him by constantly bringing up his dating history. Honestly, he's the reason the network hesitated to bring the brothers back for a second season."

"Oh, really…" Kiera's voice wavered. Rodrick's eyebrows drew together, and he mouthed the words *what's wrong?* Kiera waved a hand and focused on Tiana.

"I mean, I met Tyrone when he was still working at that radio station. He's definitely a ladies man, but I've never seen him be disrespectful or date multiple women at the same time. Still, he pissed off some woman and she's out to get him. Thankfully, we were able to clear everything up with this latest picture. I know your relationship is new, but if you're really dating then this works out perfectly for you and him. Seeing him settle down with one woman will go a long way with the viewers. People love a redeemed bad boy. You are dating…aren't you?"

Kiera hated herself but she couldn't correct Tiana. Not when a steady job that could lead to more jobs was dangling in front of her like a juicy piece of meat in front of a hungry wolf. Her kitchen drawer was filled with past-due bills and her email inbox was flooded with the notifications. She'd apologize to Tyrone later. "Y-yes…we are."

"Great! Anyway, come by the office on Monday to fill out the paperwork and sign the forms. I'm so excited about the direction this could go. It'll be great."

"Yeah…great. Thanks, Tiana." Kiera hung up and stared at the phone. What had she done? She hadn't seen or spoken with Tyrone since the wedding. She didn't know how Tiana had gone from seeing a picture of them kissing and jumped to the conclusion they were dating.

"Dammit!" Kiera snatched up her phone and searched for Tyrone's name. Sure enough, the first thing to come up was a picture of the two of them. Behind that damn bush that hadn't done its job. Her back against the wall and his thigh between her legs.

Anyone looking at that picture would assume they were dating.

Rodrick leaned forward on the couch. "What's wrong?"

She quickly clicked the button to darken her phone. If Rodrick saw it then he'd save the picture and send it to his girlfriend, their cousins and everyone else in the family. Her brother did not waste any opportunity to tease her or engage in family gossip. Her name wasn't associated with Tyrone at the moment. It was just him with "another unnamed woman" on the brief scan she'd seen. Until she figured out what to do about the lie she'd just told, she wouldn't get her brother and his wagging tongue started.

"I got the job of lead makeup artist on the *Haunted Homeboys* show."

Her brother's eyes widened. "Really! That's great, Key," he said, using her childhood nickname.

"Yeah...great." He pulled out his cell phone and started tapping away at the screen. Kiera frowned. "What are you doing?"

"Putting it in the family group chat."

Kiera's eyes widened and she reached for the phone. "No. Why?"

He jerked back his hand so she couldn't get the phone. "To celebrate. Look at you. My little duckling getting a real job in the makeup industry. I'm proud of you."

She dropped her hand and sighed. She hated the

duckling reference. Back in middle school, Rodrick's nickname for her was "ugly duckling." When he'd caught her crying and found out one of his friends used the nickname, he'd apologized, fought his friend and stopped calling her that in front of other people. She'd gotten back at him by calling him a meathead, since his grades hadn't been the best, then he'd dropped the *ugly* and just called her *duckling*. Their one unspoken rule was that they didn't use the nicknames in front of none-family members. They could tease each other, but others couldn't.

"I hope everything works out…"

"Why wouldn't it work out?" he asked as his fingers finally stopped tapped on the screen. "I've got to admit, I didn't think you'd go far with the makeup thing, but you're doing good, sis. This is big."

She smiled, appreciating her brother's words. "It is big."

Her cell phone immediately started to chime. The family group chat included their parents, aunts, uncles and cousins. She looked down at her phone. "You put it in both family chats?" There was one for both her mom's side and her dad's side of the family.

"Hell, yeah. They need to know my sister is on her way to Hollywood."

Kiera laughed. "Not quite, but maybe." She'd love to make it to LA one day. In her mind, all of her problems and bills would magically vanish if she could just break in to big-time movies and television shows. Of course, she realized that would require budgeting and money management on her part, but until she was in a place to have money to manage, she wouldn't worry about that.

"I'm going to get another beer," Rodrick said. "Want one?"

She shook her head. "Nah, I've got to finish my video."

He nodded and headed toward the kitchen. Kiera stared at all the congratulations coming through on her phone. She sighed then bit her lip. What was she going to do? She hadn't expected Tyrone to reach out to her. She understood that kiss was just a one-time thing and that night he'd been on the prowl for a one-night stand. She'd been right that in the cold light of day she'd been glad she'd stuck to her guns and avoided making another relationship mistake.

Tyrone had lit a fire and passion in her. One so hot she'd kissed him and forgotten about her reasons for breaking up with Mike, a guy who'd strung her along with "breaks" and good sex in between to avoid commitment. When they'd first started seeing each other she hadn't cared. She'd had dreams of making her makeup business grow and didn't want to be tied down. He had expectations of her being at his beck and call, and when she wasn't he'd get impatient and say he wanted to see other people. They'd played that dance for two years before Kiera knew she was done. She wasn't sure if she was ready for marriage, but she knew she wanted and deserved more than the crap she'd accepted from him.

She went back to the picture of her and Tyrone again. Would confessing that she lied and that she and Tyrone weren't dating cost her the job? How was she going to clear this up? She scrolled her contacts and remembered she didn't have Tyrone's number. She'd given him hers, but he hadn't called her, which meant she didn't have a way to let him know she'd gone along with Tiana's assumption.

She groaned and dropped her head to the couch. "What am I going to do about this?"

Chapter Five

Tyrone spotted Kiera through the window sitting in a corner near the back of the coffee-and-wine bar where they'd agreed to meet. He hurried out of the steadily falling rain into the warm interior and lowered his umbrella. The sound of smooth jazz and the low hum of conversation greeted him. Despite it being after 8:00 p.m., the place was crowded. Groups huddled in the cozy chairs settled around small, round glass-top tables and individuals filled the stools at the bar lining one side.

Kiera glanced up from her cell phone when the chime at the door rang. She raised a hand and waved him over. He wiped his feet on the mat and headed in her direction. As he drew closer, his attraction to her once again struck him like a sledgehammer.

She was dressed casually in a fitted black top and jeans that hugged her curves, with a long gray cardigan. Her short hair was gone and been replaced by a full halo of curly hair that brushed her shoulders and her makeup highlighted her cheekbones and full lips. Despite her laid-back attire, she still managed to look dazzling.

"Hey, did you have trouble finding the place?" she asked as he sat in the cushioned chair across from her.

He shook his head. "Nah, it was easy enough to find. Parking was the hard part."

"Yeah, it can be rough over here. I hope you didn't have to walk too far." She glanced at the rain sliding down the window, then back to him.

Tyrone dropped the dripping umbrella onto the floor beneath the table. "I was good." He pointed to her glass. "What are you drinking?"

"The house merlot." She picked up her wineglass and swirled the dark red liquid.

"Any good?"

She lifted a shoulder. "It's not that expensive and I like it. So, basically, it's delicious to me."

He chuckled and nodded. "Cool. Then I'll get a glass of that, too." He stood. "Need a second?"

"I'm good for now."

Tyrone went to the bar and ordered the same. Kiera seemed to be in a good mood, which was good for him. When he'd texted her to ask if they could talk she'd immediately agreed. He hoped that meant word of them being a "couple" hadn't gotten back to her. He'd been impulsive and grasping at any lifeline he could find when he'd blurted out they were together. The more he considered what he'd said after the video call, the more he'd convinced himself that the idea wasn't half-bad. If she hadn't heard, and he had the chance to sell the benefits of them pretending to be a couple, because there were benefits, then maybe she'd keep her good mood and go along with his plan.

He smiled when he went back to the table and sat across from her. She returned the gesture and took a sip of her wine. She licked her lips after pulling the glass away and Tyrone's gaze followed the reflexive movement. Memories of her mouth beneath his rushed back. Memories he'd indulged in way more than he'd expected after that night.

You're not here to hook up. Get your mind right, Tyrone!

He took a sip of his wine, which was good, and took a fortifying breath. How exactly did you broach the subject of asking a person to be your fake girlfriend?

"Thank you for agreeing to see me," he said.

"About that picture," she said at the same time.

They froze and Tyrone rubbed the back of his head. "You saw the picture?"

"Yeah… I heard it was out there and searched it up."

He cringed and thought of the various comments that accompanied the picture. Comments referring to his "community peen" and referring to her as "another notch for his bedpost." Kiera hadn't originally been identified as the woman in the picture, but it hadn't taken long for internet sleuths to figure out who she was.

"Sorry about that," he said.

She waved a hand. "I kissed you back, so it's not as if I wasn't a willing participant."

"You were willing to kiss me, but not to be dragged into a potential scandal."

She pressed a hand to her heart. "My name wasn't brought up at first. Now everyone is saying I'm your—" she glanced around the room then leaned forward and lowered her voice "—girlfriend. I want you to know that I didn't start that rumor."

He nodded and leaned in. "I know."

Relief filled her eyes. "You do? I was worried you'd think I'd started it. Tiana asked and I didn't know how to tell her—"

"I started it."

She jerked up straight. "You what?" Her voice raised to a squeak. A few people looked their way.

Tyrone grinned stiffly at the people watching them before reaching for her hand. He wrapped his fingers around hers and tugged her forward again. "Yeah...don't freak out. Let me explain."

Kiera bared her teeth in what he guessed was supposed to be a smile, then tilted her head to the side. "Explain quickly," she said between clenched teeth.

"I did this for us."

She blinked. "What *us*?"

He pointed to her chest, then his. "Us…sweetheart." He tried out the endearment to see if it would fit.

Her eyes narrowed. "Don't called me *sweetheart*." She pulled her hand.

He let her go. "Okay, I won't, but will you at least hear me out."

She picked up her wineglass, crossed her legs and sat back in her chair. "Explain." Her voice was no-nonsense as she took a sip and stared at him from over the rim of her glass.

Considering she hadn't tossed the wine in his face, or stormed out of the room in anger, he was already winning. "Alright, see, what had happened was—"

"Oh, Lord, you're about to tell a lie." She held up a hand and shook her head.

"I'm not about to tell a lie. I've already told the lie," he conceded, shrugging and giving her a don't-hate-me look that usually melted icy walls.

She twisted her lips then scoffed. "You are too much." She sighed and her shoulders relaxed. "Okay, so what happened?"

Confident that his look worked, he scooted his chair closer to hers. "Okay, if you saw the pictures then you read the comments."

"About you being a player? Yes, I read them."

"I'm not a player."

"Let me guess—you're open and honest with every woman you meet." Her voice was sarcastic and her narrow-eyed look said she already doubted any words coming out of his mouth.

"I am."

She tipped her glass at him. "Player."

"Okay, whatever. The thing is, I just haven't found the right one. I'm not against relationships, I just don't want one right now."

"Then why say I'm your girlfriend?"

"Because the network was considering canceling our show over of my reputation. You know they're big on image and family wholesomeness."

Her head tilted to the side and she gave him a sly smile. "Which means they can't have one of their up-and-coming stars slinging *D* to every woman he meets."

Tyrone narrowed his eyes. "Nobody is swinging anything." He ignored her smirk and continued. "Look, when the picture surfaced and our agent talked about them not renewing, I panicked. I said you were my girlfriend. She knew who you were and loved the idea of having a couple working together. The network wants to incorporate more of our private lives into the next season. My brothers are settled and so, they want me to be settled, too."

"So, you told everyone I was your girlfriend."

There was a question hovering in her tone of voice. The truth was right there, that they'd met and kissed, and then gone their separate ways. But the truth wouldn't have helped him, or her. The truth would have made things worse and he would have screwed up the one thing he'd accomplished that his brothers never thought he could. He would have lost the show he'd fought so hard to convince them to believe in.

"This helps us both," he said. "You wanted to work on our show and now they want you on the show. It's a win-win for everyone. Don't you think?"

"What if I was already in a relationship?"

The words only stopped him for half a second before he shrugged them off. "I wasn't worried about that."

Her lips parted in the cutest "oh" shape before she asked, "Why not?"

It was his turn to smirk after taking a sip of wine. He held up one finger. "One, because why would you kiss me like that if you were." He lifted another finger. "And two, if you were in a relationship and kissed me like that, then it wasn't one that was very serious in the first place."

Her perfectly styled eyebrows raised as she chuckled. "Oh, you've got me all figured out, huh?"

If only he could figure her out. He'd love to know

what she liked and disliked, and find ways to make her smile. The thought was too big and stirred up a feeling he didn't want to dive into and swim around with.

"No, I don't. But what I have figured out is how to make things work for the best. I want our show to succeed. I told you before I don't want to be the reason why we're canceled. You said you wanted the opportunity to be the lead makeup artist on a show on the network. Now you have that opportunity. Doing this and getting exposure during the filming of the second season will help you reach your goals. Win. Win."

He picked up his wineglass and took a sip. He watched her consider his words in silence. Instead of pushing, he savored the rich flavor of the wine. He tried to appear calm despite the racing of his heart and the dampness of his palms. If she said no, then not only would he have to admit that he'd lied and face the censure of his brothers, but the admission would also, more than likely, cost them the show. He needed her and he wasn't against begging if he had to.

"You really think this is going to work?" She sounded doubtful, but there was just enough of a spark of interest in her eyes to make him feel as if he'd get her to agree with him.

"Come on, Kiera, I know you know a good arrangement when it comes up. Look at how far the network went to make the wedding a hit. They hired seat fillers. You know they'll play up our love story and we'll both come out on top in the end. What do you say?" He tipped his glass toward her. "Will you be my fake girlfriend?"

Chapter Six

"Are you nervous?"

Kiera glanced over at Tyrone sitting in the driver's seat of his Audi sedan. He'd picked her up so they could arrive at the Exploration Network's anniversary party together. Everyone who had anything to do with the success of the network would be there, from executives to producers, show hosts and camera crews. Kiera couldn't believe she was actually going to be in the room with so many influential people. If she'd had any doubts about her decision to be Tyrone's fake girlfriend, the invitation to this party pushed them out of her mind.

"I'm not nervous. Why?"

He pointed at her lap. "Because your leg is shaking."

Kiera immediately stopped bouncing her leg. She

ran her hands across her thighs, then stopped as the material of her black sequin dress slid up her thigh. "I'm not nervous."

Tyrone gave her a reassuring smile. "Why are you nervous? It's not that big of a deal."

"Not that big of a deal? We're lying to everyone at this party."

"Don't say it like that. We're playing a part that will further our career at the Exploration Network."

She pursed her lips and considered his words before answering. "You do realize that playing a part implies not being ourselves?"

"I don't know. The attraction we felt is true. The kiss we shared was hot. This doesn't have to be a fully fake situation." He looked at her and wiggled his eyebrows.

Kiera stared for a second before laughing and shaking her head. "Please don't tell me that works on women?"

He lifted a shoulder and grinned. "I guess not. You're the only one I've tried that with."

"How about we start by getting our story straight," she said.

"What story?"

"The how-did-we-meet-and-start-dating story," she said.

He frowned. "You think people will ask us about that."

"You seriously think people won't?" Kiera asked

with a laugh. "The entire reason we were invited to this party is because people can't wait to find out if we're really dating."

"But we told them we're dating."

She reached over and patted his shoulder. He'd taken off the jacket to his suit and she could feel the hard muscle of his shoulder beneath the soft material of his dress shirt. She pulled back quickly. The key to a fake relationship was keeping the line and the reason they were doing this clear.

"You can't be that naive," she said. "The story started because you were accused of being a player and now you've suddenly got a very convenient girlfriend. They're going to want to know how we ended up together."

He stared out of the window for a while before responding. "Yeah... I guess you're right."

She stifled a smile at his petulant tone. "What were you going to say if people asked?"

"That we met at the wedding and hit it off."

"Nah, that's way too convenient. Say we originally ran into each other at the channel's headquarters or at a mutual friend's party. You asked me out."

"Why didn't you ask me out?" he said with a half grin.

"Because everyone will agree that you approached me, Slinger of Community D," she said with a wink.

Tyrone shook his head and chuckled. "Oh, you got jokes. Aight, so, I asked you out. Then you—"

"I said no."

His eyes darted from the road to her. "Why would you say no?"

"Because I heard the rumors. I wasn't sure if I believed you."

"But then I charmed you," he said in a smooth voice that slid over her and made her body shiver.

"Why did you decide to charm me out of all the women out there?"

They stopped at a red light. Tyrone turned and stared into her eyes. "Because you captivated me the moment I saw you." Even though a sexy smile hovered over his lips, there was just enough of a glint of truthfulness in his mesmerizing gaze to make her heart flip. If she didn't know that saying slick lines that made hearts flip was part of his DNA she'd believe that flip and his look were signs of something real.

She waved a finger at him. "Oh…you're good."

Tyrone grinned and faced forward. "Whatever. Is that good enough for your story?"

"It's good enough." If he looked at her like that while telling the story then he'd have no problem convincing people of what they said.

"I told my brothers that we didn't tell anyone because we just started dating a few weeks ago and weren't making a big deal about it."

"Sounds good," she said, nodding. "Are you going to be okay doing this?"

"Why wouldn't I be?"

"There aren't any women who think they're your girlfriend who are going to jump out of the wood-work and try to pull out my extensions, are there?" She ran her fingers through the sleek ebony extensions that fell to the middle of her back. Kiera loved changing her hair as much as she changed her clothes.

Tyrone waved a hand. "Nah. I broke things off with any woman I had an attachment with months ago. I told you I didn't want my dating history to be the reason why the show was canceled. I decided to take a break until the season was finished."

It wasn't lost on her that he didn't say he'd broken things off with just one woman, but with *any* woman he had a connection with. Meaning there'd been more than one in his life at the time. She'd guessed his persona correctly at their first meeting. He must have been desperate to keep his show if he was willing to cut off all his relationships and come up with a fake relationship to clean up his image.

"Why not just fake-date one of those women?"

"You were the one I was caught kissing," he said flippantly.

"Oh, right." She glanced out of the window. His admission shouldn't have made her feel so hollow. It was the truth.

"And I like you," he said after several seconds. "It was fun hanging out with you at the wedding.

I'd rather do this with you than anyone I was talking to before."

She glanced over at him, and their eyes met. A half grin still hovered around his lips. She couldn't tell if he was just being charming or if he was serious. That uncertainty didn't stop the hollow feeling she'd had from filling up. She already knew she'd have to be careful around Tyrone. If she wasn't careful, she'd easily be seduced by his sweet words and charm.

The party was just getting into full swing when Kiera and Tyrone arrived. A valet attendant parked the car and the two of them headed to the front door of the nightclub. Tyrone's hand, warm and firm, slid into Kiera's. A jolt of awareness shot up her arm. She stopped in her tracks and stared at him.

"What?" he said, lifting a shoulder. "Shouldn't we be holding hands?"

"Yeah…my bad. It was just unexpected." She'd forgotten how her body responded to his touch at the wedding.

He nodded. "I didn't mean to startle you. Is it okay?"

There was no need for her to be so jumpy. She'd agreed to this. It wasn't as if playing a part was foreign to her. She might not be an actress, but she'd pretended to be a happy guest at enough weddings and parties that she sometimes felt like one. She could play this part. If she needed a reminder of why she was here, all she had to do was think about the student loan payment that had nearly drained her bank account before Tyrone picked her up, or her rent due the following week. She could play this part and she could play it well.

She squeezed his hand. "It's fine. Let's do this."

Inside they were immediately sucked into the party. Kiera was known by a few people there thanks to her connection with Tiana, but she rarely received a lot of attention when she was a seat filler at one of these events. She wasn't a celebrity and had barely reached online-influencer status. She'd assumed some people would be interested in her and Tyrone. She had not been prepared for the level of interest.

"How did you two meet?" one of the hosts of another paranormal investigation show asked.

"You make such a cute couple!" the producer of the network's most popular cooking show enthused.

"I can't wait to see you both on the show," said Tiana, who was also the producer of *Haunted Homeboys*. Tiana was average height, curvy with dark brown skin and thick curly hair that framed her face in a perfectly symmetrical afro.

The phrases were repeated over and over during the night by various people. Tyrone soaked up the attention like a sponge dropped in the middle of a swimming pool, expanding and inflating with each line of adoration and praise. Of course, he would. His plan was working. Everyone had nothing but

great things to say about their show and now that
the threat of being canceled was gone, things should
only get better.

"Did you know that you were being filmed when
you kissed?" Tiana asked.

Kiera shook her head. "Do you think we would
have kissed there if we knew we were being filmed?"

Tiana lifted a shoulder. "People will do a lot of
things in front of a camera."

The people around them laughed. Tyrone placed
his hand on Kiera's back and rubbed as if he'd been
touching her for years. "Other people will, but not us.
If I would have known, I wouldn't have done that."
He pulled her closer to his side. "I'd never want to
embarrass Kiera like that."

The women in the group swooned. Kiera barely
stopped herself from rolling her eyes. He really knew
how to lay things on thick when needed.

"And I wouldn't want to bring any distractions to
his show," Kiera said.

A deep laugh came from behind them. They
turned and one of the network executives, Dennis
Carter, walked up. "That's good to hear." Dennis
stepped up to Kiera and Tyrone. So close that Tyrone let Kiera go and Dennis moved between them
and placed an arm around both of their shoulders.
"You know, I was worried at first that this was all a
stunt to avoid bad publicity."

"Why would you think that?" Tyrone asked. Kiera

had to give it to him—he looked and sounded as if the idea of pretending to date Kiera was the most outlandish thing he'd ever heard.

"Stranger things have happened. All sorts of things conveniently work out during show negotiations," Dennis said with a sly grin.

Kiera let out a shaky laugh. "I can imagine."

"You know we pride ourselves on the image of the stars on our network," Dennis said. "The *Haunted Homeboys* was one of our most popular shows last season. We're really excited about ways to make the show even more appealing this season."

Tyrone broke away from Dennis's grip and faced him. "What are you thinking?"

Kiera shifted until Dennis's arm dropped from her shoulder. She moved next to Tyrone, and he put his hand on the small of her back.

"We'd like to include more real-life clips of you and your brothers. Let the audience see you when you're not investigating ghosts."

Tyrone nodded. "Yeah, I remember that when we discussed the new contract."

"At first we thought it would focus mostly on Dion and Wesley, but after learning that you and Kiera are a couple and now she's working on the show, we can include clips of you two working together. Starting with the sci-fi convention near your hometown next week."

Tyrone stiffened next to her. "Are you all going to be there?"

Dennis nodded. "I'm sending a few people to record you and your brothers on the panel you have. It'll be good promo for the second season and while you're there they can get some behind-the-scenes shots of you, Dion and Wesley. And since Kiera works on the show, she can be there to do your makeup and give us a couple of shots of the newest couple." Dennis grinned at Kiera. "What do you think?"

Kiera smiled and wrapped an arm around Tyrone's waist even though inside she cringed. She'd hoped to keep up this facade only when it came to the show. Not go to Tyrone's hometown and make an appearance at a convention. Going to his hometown meant meeting his family and friends. She'd hoped to keep their lives as separate as possible, but if she was doing this, then she couldn't use the excuse of not wanting to visit his hometown to avoid getting too close to his personal life.

"I can't wait!"

Chapter Seven

Tyrone was sitting on the couch watching episodes of another paranormal investigation show on a rival channel when his phone rang next to him. He glanced down at the screen. Dion's name appeared on the screen for a video call. Tyrone paused the television and held up his phone to accept his brother's call.

"What's up, Dion?"

"Hold on, let me add Wes," Dion said quickly. A few seconds later Wes was also on screen.

Tyrone leaned back on the couch and frowned at his brothers. "Both of y'all? Is everything cool?"

Wesley nodded but Dion shook his head. "Did you hear about the cameras coming to the sci-fi convention?"

"Yeah, I saw Dennis at the network party last

night. The party I told both of you to show up for. I can't be the only one doing these promotions."

"I know," Wesley said. "I had to finish up a project for a client."

"And Vanessa already had us set up to go to a concert," Dion said. "I let everyone know that we'll be at the next event."

Tyrone shook his head. "We've got a second season so we need to make sure we are available for all preseason promotions. We can't afford to mess things up."

His brothers had been happy when they'd gotten the show, but it had always been Tyrone's dream. Though they wanted the show to do well, they'd left the promotional stuff to him. Although he was used to doing promos through his work at the radio station, sometimes he wondered if his brothers cared as much about the success of the show as he did.

Dion raised an eyebrow. "Me not going to a party isn't going to mess anything up."

Tyrone barely stopped himself from rolling his eyes. Of course, his nonpartying brother would say something like that. "You need to still network with the people involved with the show."

"Didn't I say I talked to them and said I'd be at the next one?"

Wes sighed. "Alright, that's enough. Can we get to the point of this call?"

Knowing how much Wes got tired of playing

peacemaker between him and Dion, Tyrone changed the subject. "If it's about the sci-fi convention in Myrtle Beach then we don't have to worry. We're just going to talk about the show on a panel and sign some autographs."

Wesley shook his head. "It's not just the convention. It's them coming to Sunshine Beach to get a behind-the-scenes look at us and our family."

Again, Tyrone didn't see the problem. "They did say they wanted to include that in the new season. We've always wanted to bring attention back to our hometown. This is good for us, the town and the show."

Dion stared back at Tyrone as if he'd lost his mind. "Do you not understand that they want to see us in our happy relationships? You need to tell us now if this thing with you and that Kiera girl are for real."

"What?" Tyrone frowned, thrown off by his brother's words.

"Are you really dating her or is this something you just made up on the fly the other day when you found out that kissing a strange woman at a wedding could ruin your reputation and our contract negotiations?" Dion said in his voice that meant "confess now and make this easier on all of us".

Tyrone hated that voice.

He'd planned to tell his brothers the truth when things calmed down. Planned to make things easier on everyone and explain why this was a good idea, especially now that Kiera was on board. But the disappointment on his oldest brother's face automatically made him go on the defensive. He loved Dion and would fight anyone who ever tried to harm his brother, but Dion could also be a judgmental asshole at times.

"You think I lied?" Tyrone said, trying his best to sound affronted.

Dion was unphased. "Yeah, I do. You never once mentioned dating anyone and suddenly you have a girlfriend? What about the taking your time and enjoying your freedom? All that I'm-not-ready-to-settle-down talk?"

"I met the right one. Like you said I would," he countered.

Wesley twisted his lips. "Come on, Tyrone. You can be real with us."

Wesley, too! Typically Wes was the one who remained neutral whenever Tyrone and Dion were on opposite ends. He wasn't prepared for Wes to also assume the worst.

Even if their assumption was spot-on.

He tossed aside that thought. "I am being real," Tyrone said. "We even went to the party together last night. Which y'all would have known if you'd bothered to show up. We met at the network offices one day and I asked her out. She said no, but you know me. I kept trying to charm her. By the time I got to know her I really liked her. Is it so hard to believe that I would actually like a woman enough to settle down?"

"Yeah!" they both said at the same time.

His brothers started laughing while Tyrone scowled at the screen. "Come on now. Y'all can stop. I'm serious. You'll see when we're in Sunshine Beach. She'll be there."

"We know. She's the new makeup artist," Wes said.

"She was going to come, anyway. I wanted her to meet y'all. Now I don't know. I should keep her away before you poison her against me."

Dion took a long breath. "Alright, if you're saying you're really dating her then we'll see."

Dion's fiancée, Vanessa, walked up from behind and wrapped an arm around his neck before kissing his cheek. When she noticed he was on the phone she smiled and waved. "My bad. Hey, fellas."

"Hey, Vanessa," both Tyrone and Wesley said, waving back.

Vanessa's eyes sparkled with mischief. "Tyrone, I hear you've got a girlfriend. Is this for real?"

Even Vanessa! Damn, did no one think he knew how to have a girlfriend? "Yeah, you'll meet her. She'll be working on the show and staying with me in Sunshine Beach while we're doing the convention."

"Cool. I look forward to meeting her and seeing how you swept her off her feet."

Tyrone's smile felt wooden. Everyone was going

to be watching his relationship with Kiera. He hoped they could pull it off with all the scrutiny. "Just wait until you talk to her. You'll see she's crazy about me."

"But are you crazy about her?" Vanessa said with a raised eyebrow.

Dion and Wesley both focused on Tyrone. He thought about Kiera. The way she'd stolen his breath when he first saw her and how his body responded to having her close. Not only that, but she was also funny and easy to talk to. He nodded and smiled. "Yeah. She's cool."

Shock flashed across three faces, but Dion spoke first. "Well, damn. I never thought I'd see the day but I think you *are* crazy about her."

Kiera used her left shoulder to hold her cell phone to her ear while struggling to pull her keys out of her purse. She stopped in front of the rows of mailboxes in the lobby of her apartment building. After shoving aside receipts, her umbrella, a smaller purse she used as a wallet and her makeup bag, her fingers finally landed on her key ring in the bottom corner.

"I just got home and I'm going up to pack now," she said to her brother on the other end of the line.

"How long are you going to be down there?" Rodrick asked. The sounds of music and off-key singing were in the background. When she'd asked about it earlier he'd let her know Contessa was singing while making dinner. All previous problems they'd had were forgotten and the two were blissfully happy again.

"I'll be in South Carolina for a few weeks. I'll run the team doing the makeup before the brothers' panel and then I'll stick around while they're filming scenes in their hometown. One of the first investigations is in their hometown before they move on to somewhere else." She slid the key into the lock for her mailbox.

"I'm happy for you. You're finally making big moves." Pride rang into her brother's voice.

"I'm trying to." She opened the mailbox and cringed. The box was stuffed to capacity. She tried to check it once a week, but once a week often turned into once every two or three. Still holding the phone with her shoulder, she started tugging out items packed into the box.

"Not only that, but you're also dating Tyrone Livingston. I still can't believe you didn't tell me that. Before you know it, you're going to be a celebrity."

"Not hardly," Kiera said dryly as she pulled out her mail.

"What do you mean 'not hardly'? I saw that picture of you two. I haven't seen you that into a guy in a long time."

Kiera pressed a hand to her temple for a second before resuming cleaning out her mailbox. She'd known her family would eventually see the pictures, and she hadn't looked forward to the constant teasing and questions she would get. "It's not like that."

"What do you mean 'it's not like that'? You were kissing him. What is it like?"

She froze after her brother's question. She hadn't told her family about her deal with Tyrone. She and Tyrone agreed that the fewer people who knew about their arrangement, the better. They didn't need someone's loose lips to get word back to the press or the network. Not after Dennis basically accused them of faking the relationship.

As much as she hated lying to her brother, she also knew he couldn't hold water. He was just like their dad and loved to gossip. If Kiera needed to know anything about someone in the family, one call to either of them would get her the full story. If her brother knew, then everyone in her family from Georgia to New York to Oklahoma would know.

"I mean... I'm not thinking about being big-time while dating him. I'm just enjoying being with him."

"As long as he's treating you right that's all that matters. When are you going to bring him around to meet the family?"

"Um...there's no need for him to meet the family just yet." Kiera finally got all the items out of the box. She walked over to the recycling bin and immediately began tossing the sales papers, junk mail and flyers.

"Why not? We won't hurt him." Rodrick barely masked his devious laughter.

"See, that's why I'm not bringing him around y'all. Before I know it, you'll be showing him those awful pictures of me in middle and high school."

"And?"

"And, I don't need him seeing my ugly phase."

"Girl, stop. Everyone looked weird in middle school. You grew into your looks."

A nice way of saying she looked presentable now. She appreciated him trying to pretend as if she didn't need to be embarrassed by her old pictures, even if she hadn't forgotten the days before he'd grown some empathy and stopped teasing her about her acne.

"Yeah, yeah. Don't hold your breath on meeting him. Maybe if we make it through the season then I'll consider it."

A promise she knew she wouldn't have to keep. There was no reason for her and Tyrone to continue to see each other once the season finished filming. They'd also agreed to come up with a good reason to break things off that wouldn't hurt her chances of getting a job or his chances of renewing for another season.

"I really want to meet this guy. You've sounded happy recently. I've gotta check him out and make sure he's good enough for my little duckling. Plus, you know Mom and Dad are going to be anxious to meet him."

A punch of guilt went through her at the mention of their parents. They were going to want to meet him. She hadn't talked to them about her relationship with Tyrone because lying to her parents was hard for her to do without sweating profusely, and also anytime she mentioned dating someone, her parents immediately went into when-are-you-getting-married-and-having-babies mode. They'd eventually find out. Again, her brother couldn't hold water and would break his promise to keep this secret only until she was out of town.

"Which is why I'm not telling Mom and Dad about him until we are already filming the show and they can't insist that we come over for dinner or something."

She flipped through her mail as she made her way to the elevator. Her smile dwindled with each passing second. Student loans, hospital bill from breaking her ankle, credit-card bills reflecting her maxed-out status because she'd used her credit card to cover all living expenses when she couldn't work due to the broken ankle…

Every time she thought she was getting ahead something else came up.

"Hey, I'm getting on the elevator. I'll call you back."

The singing in the background grew louder. "That's cool. I think dinner is ready. Call before you go."

"Will do. 'Bye." She ended the call and went through the bills again while the elevator went up.

In her apartment, she tossed the new stack into the drawer in the kitchen with the other bills before grabbing a bottle of water and going into her living room. Her apartment was nice. More affordable than the one she'd gotten when she'd first moved and thought she had to have the most lavish apartment out there to match her dreams of being a master makeup artist. She was still in the Paces area, but on the outskirts. The rent still was a stretch, but she could manage things if she was smart.

She plopped down on the couch and rubbed her ankle. Wearing six in heels used to be manageable before six inch heels, a storm-drain grate, and a broken ankle had proven just how precarious her living situation was. She sipped the water and drowned out any lingering remnants of guilt for lying to her family about dating Tyrone. This job would help her climb out of her financial hole. She'd pretend to be Tyrone Livingston's girlfriend and she'd do a damn good job at that. The bills stuffed in her kitchen cabinet depended on it.

Chapter Eight

Kiera rang the doorbell of the cute, two-story blue home Tyrone had given her the address to. Her stomach felt as if a dozen butterflies were having a dance party in there. She took a deep breath and patted the side of her face with the back of her hand in an effort to stop the sweat popping up along her brow without smudging her makeup.

She'd chosen to go full glam for today instead of being casual. Full face, complete with contouring, full coverage foundation, smoky eyes, lashes, eyebrows and red lipstick. She wasn't sure if the crews from the network would arrive before her, and she didn't want to be caught unprepared. She'd dressed in fitted dark pants, a short-sleeved, asymmetrical white blouse and six-inch strappy heels. If anyone saw her today, they'd never imagine her as the awkward, unattractive girl in the pictures her brother loved showing off.

The door swung open, and Tyrone stood on the other side. Kiera returned his welcoming smile as he pushed open the glass storm door.

"Did you have any trouble finding the place?" He reached for the suitcase in her hand.

Kiera shook her head and followed him into the foyer. "Nope. The GPS led me straight here."

He stopped in the foyer and faced her. He'd dressed nicely, too, in a pair of stylish jeans and a short-sleeved, blue-and-white-patterned, button-up shirt. His mustache and goatee looked freshly trimmed and his hair was brushed to a lustrous, wavy shine.

"The crew hasn't gotten here yet. They mentioned they may not come to the house tonight, so we have time to get situated," he said.

"No problem." She glanced around the inside of the foyer. "You've got a nice place."

He shook his head. "It's not just mine. This is the house me and my brothers grew up in. My brother Dion used to live here until he moved to Charlotte. Now we all keep it up and take care of it. Come on in the family room."

She followed him to the family room, where a comfortable sectional sofa sat in the middle of the room facing a television over the fireplace. "I thought we were staying at your place. I wouldn't have brought my bag."

"We're staying here. I let my place go after we got the show. I stay here whenever I'm in town."

"Ah, okay."

"I'll put your stuff in the guest bedroom. Unless, you want to sleep in the room with me," he said with a cocky smile.

Kiera rolled her eyes. "Remember when we said we were going to be a fake couple. Sleeping in the same room with you will only make this thing harder."

He plopped down in the corner of the sectional. "In what way?"

"You know what way." Kiera sat next to him. "We are not going to blur the lines. That was the deal."

"I know," he said. "I'm sorry if I made you uncomfortable."

"You didn't." He'd only made her yearn for more. To spend the night lying next to him, to feel the heat of his body pressed against hers. To have his lips brush across hers again.

Their eyes met and she sucked in a breath. The teasing smile on his face faded as he watched her. She wondered if he was having the same thoughts as her.

"So, you grew up here," she said, breaking the moment.

He nodded and shifted, bending his leg so that it rested on the couch. "Yeah, after my parents died,

Dion, the oldest, dropped out of college to come back home and keep us together."

"I didn't know about your parents," she said solemnly. "I'm sorry."

"We didn't make a big deal out of it as part of the show. With the focus on the town and us, I think we'll probably touch on it more this season."

"And are you okay with that? Talking about your parents, I mean."

He nodded. "Yeah, I'm good with talking about them. I'm glad Dion stepped in when he did and kept us together. Even though it was hard."

"I'd imagine it would be. How old were you?"

"I'd just started high school and Wes was a sophomore."

"Dion couldn't have been much older?" He was the oldest but she was sure he was only four or five years older than Tyrone.

"He wasn't. He didn't get to finish a full year before the accident. When he came home, I didn't make it easy. I missed my parents, especially my mom. She always called me her little man. Her baby. I'll admit she spoiled me. It was a shock to lose her and realize that no one would ever love me as much as she did."

Tyrone glanced at her then looked away. He appeared embarrassed to have admitted as much.

"I feel the same way about my dad," she confessed. "My brother is the oldest and I'm the baby of the family. No matter what I went through or how people treated me, my dad always said I was his beautiful princess. He still does," she said with a smile.

"I went from being my mom's favorite, because even though Dion and Wes won't admit it, I was the favorite," he said with a wistful smile, "to being raised by my older brother. We bumped heads a few times, but Wesley kept us straight and we got through."

"You didn't get along?"

"Dion has always been the role model. The good one that everyone looked up to. I was the impatient hothead. So, when he came home and tried to step into my dad's shoes…let's just say I didn't take his advice to heart."

Kiera could only imagine. She tried to think about how she would have reacted if Rodrick was suddenly the head of the household. If she'd been expected to look to him for guidance or treat him as a guardian back when they were still teenagers, she doubted they would have survived a month before they tried to kill each other. She empathized for what had to be a difficult situation and admired how Tyrone and his brothers had come out on the other side with their relationships intact.

"I can understand how hard it must have been back then. Now it seems as if you and your brothers really care about each other."

"There's no one else I'd fight for like I will for them. Is it the same with you and your brother?"

She lifted one shoulder. "I mean, yeah. He's my brother and I love him. I'd do what I can to help him, but I don't know if we're as close as you and your brothers."

"Why not?"

"My brother went through an asshole phase when we were younger. He's outgrown it, but I still see hints of it every once in a while."

Tyrone laughed. "Didn't we all have an asshole phase when we were younger?"

"Some more than others," she said.

"I wonder if that's the way Dion feels about me," he said thoughtfully. "I know I didn't make things easy on him."

"I doubt it. On the show Dion comes across as very sensible. I, on the other hand, am quite petty."

Tyrone's eyebrows shot up. "Oh, really. Good to know."

"Why is that?"

"Because it means I need to work extra hard to keep you satisfied. Hell hath no fury like a petty person," he said with a wink.

Kiera laughed and playfully slapped his arm. His hand shot out and wrapped around her wrist. Their eyes met and Kiera forgot the point of their conversation. He continued to smile as he lazily ran a finger over her pounding pulse. Just like that, he had her caught in the intensity of his gaze.

Kiera pulled her hand away. He didn't hesitate to

let her go. The lingering tingle from his light touch remained.

The doorbell rang before either of them could say something. Kiera was both relieved and irritated by the interruption. She wanted to talk to him more, but being alone with Tyrone was also bringing out how easily she could be pulled in by their mutual attraction.

Tyrone pointed toward the front of the house. "I'll get that."

After he walked out of the room, she stood and took a deep breath. She needed to move around and expel the energy he'd ignited in her with one touch. Most definitely needed separate rooms with that guy.

"Dion, what are you doing here?" Tyrone's surprised voice carried to the family room.

"What do you think? We're staying here," Dion's deep voice replied.

Kiera's eyes widened and she spun toward the door. His brother was staying there, too.

There was a second of silence before Tyrone's stunned reply. "I didn't know that."

"Where did you think we'd go? Wesley's condo."

"I mean, Kiera is here," Tyrone said in a strained voice.

"That's fine. Her and Vanessa can get to know each other," Dion replied.

"Yeah," a woman, presumably Vanessa, said. "I can't wait to meet her. Is she here already?"

"Um…yeah, she's in the family room."

Kiera heard the sound of footsteps hurrying down the hall before Dion and his fiancée, Vanessa, filled the doorway. Behind them, Tyrone threw her an apologetic look.

"My bad, I didn't know they were staying," he said.

"It's no problem," Kiera said, grinning. It was definitely a problem. Where was she going to sleep now? "It's your family home. Dion, Vanessa, it's great to meet you." She slipped into the role of a new girlfriend happy to meet the family.

Vanessa came over and gave her a hug. "I'm so happy to meet you. I want to know everything. How you met and how Tyrone convinced you to give him a chance."

"Hey," Tyrone said.

Kiera and Vanessa laughed. "I'll be sure to give you all the details."

Dion rubbed his stomach. "We can get the details over dinner. I'm tired and need to change before the crew gets here. Are you taking the master bedroom?"

Tyrone shook his head. "Nah, that's your room."

Dion nodded. "I'm not going to argue against the king-size bed. You and Kiera can have the guest bedroom. I'm sure you two won't mind snuggling up in a queen."

Kiera's face heated. Her and Tyrone in a queen bed? Heaven help her!

* * *

The closing credits of the movie *Knives Out* came onto the screen and Tyrone nodded slowly. He glanced at Kiera sitting next to him on the couch. She raised an eyebrow and gave him an expectant look. He turned from her to the eager expressions of Dion and Vanessa curled up together on the opposite end of the sectional sofa.

"Alright, ya'll were right. It's a good movie," he conceded.

When Tiana had called to say that she and the cameraman were delayed due to an accident on the road and were going straight to their hotel instead of coming to see the brothers at their family home, they'd decided to watch a movie after they'd eaten.

Kiera clapped while his brother and soon-to-be sister-in-law laughed. Kiera poked his shoulder with a finger. "Told you you'd enjoy it."

"I can't believe you've never seen it," Dion said.

Tyrone shrugged. "I didn't know what it was about. The previews looked boring."

Kiera scoffed and rolled her eyes. "Whatever, previews looked boring, you admitted yourself you avoided it on purpose because so many people raved about Chris Evans in a sweater."

"Well, that was what I mostly heard the women down at the station talk about," he said. "I'm not afraid to admit when I was wrong."

"Good to know," Kiera said with a wink.

Tyrone reached over and tugged on her ear. "Oh, really. You expect me to be wrong a lot?"

She lightly slapped away his hand. "Not a lot, but at least I know you'll listen to reason."

She smiled at him and an unfamiliar sensation swirled in his chest. She'd gotten along great with Vanessa and Dion, telling funny stories about her work as a makeup artist and asking them insightful questions about what they do. She was attentive in ways he hadn't been prepared for. Like remembering that he'd picked the onions out of his salad at the wedding, and reminding Vanessa to say "no onions" on the supreme pizza she'd ordered for them to eat during the movie. He'd been touched by that small thoughtful moment more than he'd expected.

Tyrone turned quickly toward the television. "What do you want to watch next?"

"Oh, no," Vanessa said, stifling a yawn. "I'm usually in bed by now. I think I'm going to call it a night."

Tyrone glanced at his watch. It had just turned nine. "You're going to bed already?"

"You forget I'm a morning anchor. Early to bed and early to rise."

"Same for me, bruh," Dion said, stretching his arms out. "I'm still an early bird. Plus, we've got to be at the convention center early tomorrow. Tiana wants to meet us there and get some shots of us at the panelists' breakfast before filming Kiera doing our makeup before our panel later in the day."

Tyrone wasn't ready to go to bed. He was a night owl, typically staying up to midnight on weeknights, or later on the weekends. He turned to Kiera, hoping she would want to stay up, but she had her hand over her mouth covering her own yawn.

"You, too?" He tried not to sound too let down, but he wasn't ready to call it a night. Not only because he wasn't tired, but also because of the change in sleeping arrangements. The night was going to be torture, having Kiera so close to him but knowing he couldn't pull her into his arms. He'd prefer to stay up as late as possible so he could fall asleep quickly without focusing on temptation.

"Yeah. It's been a long day," she said sheepishly.

Tyrone picked up the remote. "Well, I can stay up and watch television some more then come up."

Dion shook his head. "Nah, we've got a busy day. You know you get cranky if you wake up early without a lot of sleep. Let's all call it a night."

Tyrone immediately wanted to argue—his automatic reaction whenever Dion became authoritative and started telling him what to do. He opened his mouth to do just that but caught Kiera's eye. She shook her head and slipped the remote from his hand.

"If you're tired then I'll have to use more makeup on you." She softened the words with a small, cute smile.

His frustration with Dion melted as he stared into her warm brown eyes. Accepting that he was out-numbered, and continuing to argue would only bring questions he didn't want to answer, Tyrone sighed and nodded. "Fine. We'll all call it a night."

They cleaned up the plates and cups they'd used while watching the movie before making their way upstairs. Dion and Vanessa wished them good-night and disappeared behind the door of the master bed-room. Once he and Kiera were inside his old room, he glanced around before his eyes settled on the queen-size bed.

"Um… I can sleep on the floor," he offered. He didn't want to sleep on the floor. His bed was com-fortable, and the floor was not, but he'd do it if she was uncomfortable sharing the bed with him.

Kiera shook her head. "I'm not going to put you on the floor. We can share the bed."

He perked up. "Oh, really."

She held up a finger. "Just to sleep. Besides, it'll be weird and tip your brother off if we bring in extra blankets to put you on the floor."

"Are you sure?" He pressed a hand to his chest. "I just want to make sure you can control yourself with me in bed next to you."

Kiera looked skyward and laughed so easily his ego was bruised. "Not hardly." She went to her bag in the corner. "Where's the bathroom? I'd like to shower before bed."

"Down the hall to the right."

She pulled out a small orange bag that he assumed held toiletries and a pair of pajamas. He couldn't tell much about the pajamas except there were two pieces that looked completely modest, to his disappointment. Stupid, since he wouldn't be able to sleep a wink if she was next to him in any type of sexy nightwear.

"I'll be right back."

Tyrone nodded. "I'll get my stuff out and shower after you."

He watched her leave then went to his bag and pulled out the items he'd need to shower. He typically slept naked, but doubted Kiera would appreciate that if they were sharing a bed. As much as he would love to lie next her naked, to have her smooth skin and soft curves all pressed against his body, he wasn't going to be an asshole. As much as his body wanted Kiera, his brain acknowledged she was doing him a favor and he didn't need to ruin that.

Kiera came back into the room several minutes later. Tyrone looked up from scrolling his phone and jerked back. "What the hell is that?" He pointed at her face.

She glared through the slits of the white paper covering her features. "It's a moisturizing mask, thank you very much."

"You wearing that all night? I mean, I investigate ghosts but it doesn't mean I want to sleep next to one."

She crossed the room and hit his shoulder. "Stop it."

"I'm serious. I'll have nightmares." He tried not to grin but couldn't help himself.

She laughed and went to her bag, where she pulled out some lotion. "No, I'm not wearing it all night. Though I should because you're giving me a hard time."

"You know what, it's beautiful. Moisturize all you need while I'm in the shower. No hard time from me." He circled his face with his index finger. "Just lose the Casper mask before bed."

Kiera picked up a pillow and tossed it at him. He hurried out the door before she could hit him. Tyrone chuckled on his way to the bathroom. He showered quickly and hoped it would give her enough time to take off the mask. He wouldn't really have nightmares, but he'd much prefer to see Kiera's face free of the paper covering if he woke up in the middle of the night.

When he went back into the room, he froze. Every light was off. Just a hint of moonlight through the window illuminated the room.

"Kiera? Are you asleep already?" he asked.

"No, I just turned off the lights when I got in bed. My bad—do you need the light?"

"Nah, I'll be okay." He knew his room like the

back of his hand, so he made his way over to the bed and slipped beneath the covers.

Kiera was all the way to the edge of her side of the bed, but he still felt the heat of her body as if she was pressed against him. "Are you good? You've got enough room?"

"Yeah. I'm good."

After a few moments, she spoke again. "Dion and Vanessa are really nice. I had fun hanging out with them."

"Yeah, I did, too."

She turned toward him and scooted closer. "You say that as if you're surprised."

"I don't hang out with Dion and Vanessa a lot."

"Why not?"

"Well, Vanessa didn't like me when we first met."

Kiera leaned up on an elbow. "What? Why not?" The room was dark, so he couldn't make out her features, but he could picture the look of shock and interest on her face.

"We were investigating her grandmother's house and she thought we were scam artists. I thought she would ruin our chance at getting a show. It took a while, but we eventually learned to get along."

"But you still don't hang out together?"

"I hang out with Dion. I think they've gone to dinner with Wes and his girlfriend, Cierra, before. I never wanted to be the third wheel. I guess it is kind of fun to have a girlfriend."

He heard her soft laughter and like a moth to a flame, he scooted even closer to her.

"Why were you investigating her grandmother's house?" she asked softly.

"Her grandmother believed her husband was haunting the place."

Kiera gasped and reached out a hand. Her fingers brushed across his chest, covered in a T-shirt for modesty, but he wished they were on his skin. "Was he?"

"Yeah, but not for the reason she thought."

"What was the reason?"

Tyrone spent the next few minutes telling Kiera about the investigation at Vanessa's grandmother's home. From there she asked other questions. How they got started and why they enjoyed helping people find out why the ghosts were hanging around in their homes. He asked her questions about her family, learned that she loved the R&B singer Jessica and in all her wedding adventures she really hadn't found a flavor of cake she disliked. When she finally yawned and rolled over, he instinctively reached out his arm, wrapped it around her waist and pulled her back against his front.

Kiera stiffened. "What are you doing?"

"My bad." He lifted his arm. "I just wanted to hold you."

She was quiet for a heartbeat, then seemed to relax. "I'm okay with that." Her voice was soft and sleepy.

Smiling, Tyrone pulled her close against him. He

kissed her shoulder and breathed in the sweet scent of her. Within seconds the comfort of her body against his lured him to sleep.

Chapter Nine

Kiera woke up before Tyrone. She'd fallen asleep in his arms and, despite moving during the night, he'd still been holding her when her eyes opened early that morning. She quickly slipped out of bed. As much as she wanted to linger in his embrace and enjoy the warmth and comfort of his body cradling hers, she also didn't want to run the risk of him seeing her without makeup. Silly and superficial, maybe, but she wasn't perfect. It had taken her years to try and feel confident in her own skin. Currently, that confidence came with not letting anyone see her naked face. She still bore the scars of those hard teenage years, both mentally and physically, and she didn't owe anyone access to either.

After she showered, did her makeup and dressed

in a pair of black pants and a black top to avoid stains, since she'd be doing the brothers' makeup later that day, she went downstairs in search of coffee. Tyrone had mumbled that he was getting up before he'd rolled over and pulled the covers over his head when she mentioned going down. She hoped he did get up soon. They had to drive the hour to the Myrtle Beach Convention Center for the pre-convention breakfast.

The smell of coffee greeted her in the kitchen. Dion and Vanessa were sitting at the kitchen table, both fully dressed, Dion in a pair of dark slacks and a gray top and Vanessa in a cute, fitted blue sundress. They sipped coffee and scrolled through their phones. Despite their preoccupation with their phones, their feet overlapped and rubbed against each other beneath the table.

They both looked up and smiled when Kiera came into the kitchen. "Good morning!" Vanessa said in a bright voice.

"Morning. You both are up early," Kiera said.

Vanessa shrugged. "I can barely sleep past five in the morning."

"Same for me," Dion said. He glanced at his watch. Kiera knew it had to be close to six thirty based on when she'd gotten up and dressed. "Is Tyrone up?" he asked, skepticism thick in his deep voice.

Kiera shook her head as she went over to the coffee machine. "He barely cracked his eyelids when I told him I was heading downstairs."

"That sounds like Tyrone," Dion said with a shake of his head. "He was never a morning person. I always had to fight him to get up in time for school."

"If he's not moving soon then I'll get him moving." Kiera poured coffee into a black ceramic mug.

"Good, because I don't want to be late. I'm already nervous as it is."

"I don't know why," Kiera said. "You and your brothers are so great on the show. It's just the three of you being yourselves and talking about doing what you love."

"On the show there isn't a crowd of people looking and staring. I really want to get there in time for the participants' breakfast to hear any suggestions they make before we go over the filming needs with the rest of the crew. Not to mention the three of us agreed to sign promotional items before the event." Dion glanced down at his watch again and his lips tightened.

Vanessa ran a hand over his shoulder. "It'll be okay. We'll make it in time. The convention center is an hour away and the breakfast isn't until nine."

"You know what, I'll go nudge Tyrone now," Kiera said quickly. The tension that appeared on Dion's face as he talked about the upcoming day was all the prompting she needed. Tyrone might be cool and confident when it came to putting on a show, but his older brother obviously was not. Knowing their history of butting heads, she didn't want an argument to break out.

Coffee mug in hand, she hurried back upstairs. If she had to snatch the covers off Tyrone and force him out of bed then that's what she'd do. A smile spread across her lips at the thought of messing with him this early. He liked to tease her and she enjoyed teasing him back.

She opened the door to the bedroom and expected to see Tyrone still buried beneath the covers. Instead, he was very much awake, and nearly naked. Nothing but a flimsy pair of boxers covered his body. He stopped rummaging through his bag of clothes and stared at her.

She couldn't help it. Her eyes moved before her brain could issue the no-ogling command. Her gaze traveled down the length of his chest. He wasn't overly muscular but toned just enough for her to know he spent some time in the gym. Red boxers barely concealed the rigid length of the erection straining against the slit at their front.

Kiera's breathing faltered and her eyes widened. Again, her body responded before her brain could function and she pointed at the front of his boxers. "What's going on?"

Tyrone glanced down then looked up. He shifted and held the clothes he'd pulled out of his bag in front of him. "It happens every morning. What are you doing back up here?"

Heat filled her cheeks. Yes, she knew that guys often woke up with erections. Knowing the physiological fact didn't do anything to stop her body from having its own biological response. Or keep her from acting like a blushing virgin. "Your brother. He's, um, ready to go soon. I was sent to wake you up."

He nodded then went back to rummaging through his bag. "I figured he'd be ready. I meant it when I said I would get up soon."

"I just wanted to be sure. I'll go and let you get dressed." The words came out, but her feet refused to move. The man was gorgeous and it was hard to tear her eyes away.

"You don't have to run out. Unless all of this is too much for you to handle." He finished the sentence with a sexy wink.

The wink and words snapped her out of her trance. She cocked her head to the side and smirked. "I believe I'm the one who'll be too much for you to handle."

"Oh, really?" he said, crossing his arms over his chest.

Damn, why did his biceps have to bulge like that? She jerked her thoughts from his biceps back to the conversation. "Really. I've been known to make men speak in tongues."

His eyes widened. "Oh, have you?"

She lifted a shoulder. "It's true." She sipped her coffee and watched him over the rim. The conversation was going into territory it didn't belong, but damn, if the man was hard not to flirt with.

The spark of humor in his eyes flared into something hot and alluring. "Well, I hate to brag, but I have made women completely forget how to speak."

Kiera pursed her lips. "Seriously? That's your comeback?"

"What? I'm for real. One woman is still in a trance," he said in a serious voice.

She burst out laughing. "You are unbelievable. Once again, I don't understand how you managed to pull women with those lines."

A grin spread across Tyrone's face. "It's the confidence. That gets you a long way."

He walked toward her with a bundle of what looked like another pair of underwear in his hands and his toiletry bag. He stopped in front of her, and Kiera fought with the urge to run her fingers across the hairs on his chest.

"Are you hoping that confidence eventually works on me?"

He shook his head. "Nah. I want you to sleep with me when you're sure about sleeping with me. No questions. No doubts about the outcome. Just you and me—" he ran a finder down her bare forearm "—doing what we both want to do."

His voice lowered to a sexy whisper that slid

across her skin just as deliciously as his light caress. The touch on her arm echoed through every part of her body. Her nipples tightened and wetness slid between her legs.

Damn, he was so very good at this.

Kiera stepped back and his finger fell away. Her body was on high alert and screamed for her to toss him on the bed, rip of her clothes and ride him like a cowgirl. "We'll be waiting for your downstairs."

She hurried out of the room before she caved in to the craving to do everything she wanted to do to Tyrone Livingston.

The preconvention breakfast was packed. The cameras from the Exploration Network were set up to get the perfect shots of Tyrone and his brothers. Even the few celebrities the convention organizers were able to pull in for the event were there.

Tyrone should be on cloud nine. People recognized the "Haunted Homeboys" and were excited about their panel. It was more than he'd ever wanted. He was happy. On cloud seven and a half or eight, instead of nine. He couldn't get to nine, because he was horny as hell and couldn't do a damn thing about it.

Every time he looked at Kiera, he remembered the heat that flashed in her eyes and the way the tip of her tongue flickered across her full lower lip, as if she wanted to taste him when he'd flirted with her that morning. He'd spent half the morning trying to focus on something else to keep from rising like a tuning fork. He hadn't had this problem since sixth-grade math, when Stephany Hampton used to wear those tiny shirts that always rose and gave a sneak peak of her belly button whenever she raised her hand.

Just like back then, his face flamed, and he wanted to run from the room with embarrassment. He was sure everyone there could see how much he wanted to pounce on his girlfriend. They'd understand, of course, and probably would expect him to do just that. Except, she wasn't really his girlfriend and like a dumbass he'd agreed to her suggestion that they don't sleep together while doing this.

He shouldn't have teased her like that. She'd stepped away and hurried out of the room, so he'd obviously made her uncomfortable, despite the moment of consideration in her eyes. He'd gotten himself all hot and bothered over something he couldn't follow up on. The season hadn't officially started filming and he was already breaking the rules. He'd be lucky if they got through this without Kiera slapping him in the face.

Wesley slapped him on the shoulder. "You good?"

Tyrone jumped and turned to his brother sitting next to him at the table. "Yeah. Why?"

"You keep frowning like something is wrong." He leaned in. "Did you and Kiera fight?"

Tyrone shook his head. "Nah, nothing like that. Why would you think that?"

"Because you two are stiff and barely talking to each other. I just want to make sure you're not about to break up right before the season starts filming."

"We're not. It's good. We're good." He turned away from Wes and leaned to Kiera at his left. "Hey, can we go somewhere and talk?"

She turned to him with a frown. "What's wrong?"

"Nothing—please smile," he said, smiling at her. Her face immediately cleared, and she smiled back at him as if she was really in love with him, and his heart stuttered for a second. "Just a quick talk before we go into the next thing."

She nodded. "Sure, babe."

His eyebrows rose. "Babe?"

She cocked her head to the side. "Bae?"

He cringed and shook his head. "Definitely not."

She laughed and the tightness in his chest lifted a little. If she was still teasing and laughing with him then maybe she didn't full-on hate him. He took her hand in his and led her from the table. When Dion asked where they were going, he said they'd be right back.

He led her out of the room and into the hallway, far away from the door. When they were out of earshot of others he spoke. "I'm sorry."

Her eyebrows drew together, and confusion filled her eyes. "For what?"

"For what I did and said earlier. I was out of line, and I made you uncomfortable. You're doing me a favor and I should remember that and follow the rules you set out."

Her eyes widened before she smiled. "You're actually apologizing?"

"I told you I admit when I'm wrong. I was out of line and I'm sorry. Wes commented about how we seemed stiff, and it made me feel worse. I don't want you to feel uncomfortable while we do this."

"I appreciate that, but…" She lowered her voice. "Can I tell you something?"

"Sure."

She stepped closer. "I wasn't uncomfortable because of what you said, I was uncomfortable about how much I wanted to throw out my own rule."

He swallowed hard. She was not making this easy. Here he was trying to be responsible and tell her that he wouldn't come on to her, and she had to go and admit that she was having just a hard a time as he was. "Does that mean we can…?" His voice lifted in anticipation, along with his shoulders.

She held up a hand and shook her head. "No, we can't. We haven't even started filming. We can't mess this up."

"How will that mess things up?" If anything, he could only see how this would make things better.

"Have you ever had things end well when the chemistry was this hot with someone?"

He'd never felt chemistry this hot with someone before. Had she? A punch of jealousy, unexpected and potent, tightened the muscles in his stomach. He didn't want to believe there was any other man who made her want him just as much as his body craved her.

Movement to his left caught his attention. He turned and his body iced over. Sheri Thomas, aka Li'l Bit, and her cousin, Cora, had stopped in their tracks to glare at him and Kiera.

He would forever regret the day that he'd slept with Sheri and continued their friends-with-benefits relationship for as long as he had. He'd known Sheri was back in town because of her mother's health and had tried to stay away, but when she insisted she could keep things casual the head below his belt overruled the one on his shoulders and he'd gone there with a woman he used to consider a friend. Now, she hated him and had even scratched up his car after they were done with each other—something both Dion and Wesley never let him live down.

Sheri and Cora were both wearing the red volunteer T-shirts for the event, which explained their presence. The convention was suddenly going to be long and tedious as hell if he had to deal with those two.

Kiera glanced from him to the women and then back. When they continued to stare, Kiera gave a tight smile and lifted her hand to wave. "Um…hey?"

Li'l Bit blinked and gave Kiera a half smile. "Hey. We're on our way to the participants' breakfast."

She glanced at Tyrone and the frost returned to her gaze. "Tyrone."

He nodded. "Sheri."

Her cousin smirked. "Hey, Tyrone. Aren't you going to introduce us?"

Tyrone's shoulders tightened. "She's my girlfriend, Kiera. Kiera, this is Sheri and her cousin, Cora. I knew them growing up."

Sheri raised an eyebrow and Cora scoffed. "Nice to meet you, Kiera," Cora said with a twist of her lips. "I hope you have fun while in town. Be careful, though. Some people will definitely deceive you." She glared pointedly at Tyrone.

Sheri elbowed her cousin. "Let's go. See y'all around." She grabbed her cousin and pulled her off.

"I hope he treats her better than he treated you," Cora said loud enough for them to hear.

Tyrone closed his eyes and suppressed a groan. He looked back at Kiera. "Look, about that…about her."

Kiera held up a hand. "No need to explain. I'm your fake girlfriend, remember? You owe me no explanations about your past. As long as you're not sleeping with her now. Are you?"

He shook his head so hard his neck hurt. "Hell nah."

Her shoulders relaxed. She took a deep breath before pasting on a smile. "Then that's all I need to know. Now, let's go inside and show everyone what a loving boyfriend you are."

She slid her hand in his and squeezed. Tyrone squeezed hers back. He should've felt relief as she led him back into the room, but he couldn't ignore the lingering need to explain himself. To make sure Kiera understood there was absolutely nothing going on between him and Sheri, and that Cora was out of line. Even though she said she didn't care, and he was relieved she hadn't gotten dramatic about the entire thing, he didn't want Kiera to have any doubts about him, even as his fake girlfriend.

Chapter Ten

The camera focused on Kiera as she completed the final touches of Tyrone's makeup. They were in one of the prep rooms for the sci-fi convention with his brothers, the cameraman, Dorian, and Tiana. The brothers didn't really need makeup for the panel discussion, but since the network wanted shots of Kiera working with Tyrone they'd patiently sat through Kiera's efforts so the cameraman could get good shots.

Kiera stopped blending the foundation on Tyrone's chin and used the back of her hand to cover up her yawn. Tyrone's eyebrows knitted together, and concern filled his eyes.

"Tired?"

She shook her head to clear her drowsy fog. "Sorry. I didn't get much sleep last night."

"I noticed," Tyrone said. "There was a lot of tossing and turning before I fell out like a light."

There was a cough followed by a snicker from Dorian. Kiera glanced over at him. Dorian was short and thick with a pleasant face and welcoming smile. When he saw her questioning look, he had the decency to look away. She glanced at his brothers and Tiana. They also had silly looks on their faces. Realization hit. Did they assume her "tossing and turning" was because she and Tyrone spent the night making love?

Her face flamed but she looked back at Tyrone. "I know you were. Sorry for keeping you up so late." She gave him a wink for good measure. If they were going to sell this fake dating, then pretending as if she and Tyrone had a passionate relationship would only help their cause.

The truth was the chemistry between them was exactly why she'd had a hard time sleeping. How was she supposed to rest comfortably with Tyrone next to her? His warm embrace and the way he held her, as if that was enough when she knew it wasn't—at least for her—made her shift until his arm fell away. Then she'd shifted again because she missed him and he'd reach over and rested his hand on her as if to comfort her. Which only made her want to be held and she'd shuffled to a new position. Whenever he'd turned, wrapped an arm around her waist and pulled her back against him, she'd felt the rise of his erection against her behind, which just lead her to another round of tossing and turning.

True to his word, he'd respecting her wishes. He said he only wanted to hold her and that's all he did. That only made her want him even more.

Tyrone didn't miss a beat. "I didn't mind at all. You can keep me up anytime." The smile that crossed his face melted her insides and would convince anyone watching that they'd worn themselves out in each other's arms.

Her heart pumped out a dozen beats in what felt like a millisecond. She sucked in a breath and tried to focus on finishing his makeup. Hard to do. The light hit his eyes just right to turn the brown into a golden, whiskey color and his smoldering gaze remained focused on her. "I bet you will," she murmured.

Dorian chuckled. "The chemistry between you two is smoking-hot. Nothing you said would violate the censors but the way you look at each other... I can't believe people thought you were faking this relationship."

Kiera dropped her brush in Tyrone's lap. He placed his hand over hers and gently squeezed before using his other hand to give her back the brush. "Nothing is fake about the way I feel about her."

Kiera's eyes met his. Embers of desire flashed in his eyes, along with the whisper of something indefinable. Something that called to the yearning in her heart and challenged it to forget the good sense in her head.

"You know what would be good." Tiana's eager voice interrupted. "If after Kiera blends your makeup, she then gives you a quick kiss. You two are already heating up the screen with just the looks you're giving. Go ahead and add that extra bit."

Kiera straightened and turned to the producer. "But I'm done."

Tiana waved a hand. "It's fine. We'll edit it all together and you won't be able to tell. Just pretend as if you're applying his makeup and then lean in for a quick peck. Remember this is family television so it doesn't have to be a long or passionate kiss, just something to make our viewers smile or sigh."

She squeezed the brush in her hand "Um...sure." Kiera looked back at Tyrone. She expected him to look smug or self-satisfied with the idea of her kissing him for the camera. Instead, concern remained in his eyes.

"You good with doing that?" he asked.

There he went being considerate again and making her heart flutter. If she didn't want to go through with this, he'd move on and insist they film something else. Saying she was uncomfortable was exactly what she should do. She was having a hard enough time keeping her promise to herself to not fall for Tyrone's charm. But this is what she'd signed up for, and not showing some level of affection on camera would come across weird.

Okay, tell yourself this is just for the camera, the wicked voice of her libido whispered.

"I'm good," she said quickly. "It's just a small kiss for the camera. All real kisses will be just between us."

His nostrils flared and desire flashed hot, melting away the hesitation in his eyes. "I like the sound of that."

She'd worry about clarifying her words later. There would be no real kisses in their future. Ignoring the feeling of lying to herself, she focused on blending the makeup while the camera focused on her. After a few seconds, she lowered the brush and leaned in. Her lips brushed across Tyrone's. She really did plan to make it quick. She even pulled back after the quick peck. But her lids lifted, and her eyes met his. The need in his gaze was so raw and unfiltered that her body responded. His eyes narrowed at the same time she leaned in for another kiss.

This kiss was more of a slow savor than the unsatisfactory brush from before. His hand still held hers. His fingers tightened around her wrist and pulled ever so slightly. Unable to deny the pull, Kiera leaned in closer. Her other hand rested on his shoulder as their lips pressed together, then broke apart slightly, only to come together in another sensual caress. His tongue slipped out and across her lower lip. Kiera sighed just as someone coughed.

"He said it was a family show," Dion said, his voice ringing out.

Kiera jumped back and placed a hand over her tingling lips. Heat spread across her face and body, and she took a deep breath to try and slow her pounding heart. "Sorry."

"My bad," Tyrone said, his voice gruff and thick.

Dion grinned and shook his head. "No apology needed. It's great to see you two are so into each other. Dorian's right. I don't know who thought this was fake, but obviously they haven't seen you two together."

Kiera turned away from Tyrone and put her brush in her makeup bag. Tyrone stood and shifted to the side, creating more space between them. It didn't matter—she could feel his presence and she was helplessly pulled in by him.

"We should go ahead and go to the room for our panel," Tyrone said.

Tiana looked at her watch. "You're right. We can follow up with more behind the scenes of all you lovebirds later. For now, let's go ahead and get to the reason we're here."

Kiera focused on putting up her materials while the brothers shuffled out of the room. A hand rested on her waist when she thought everyone had left. She jerked up and turned to Tyrone.

"You didn't have to do that."

She shrugged and tried to pretend as if she wasn't dying to crawl back into his arms. "It would've made things worse to argue the reasons I couldn't kiss you."

He half smiled. "I look forward to the for-real kiss later. If it comes." His hand on her waist tightened for a second before he turned and left the room.

Kiera placed a hand over her heart. How was she supposed to hold out? The man hit all her buttons.

She was just finishing putting up her items when the door to the prep room opened. The woman Tyrone introduced as Sheri entered. Sheri with the cousin who had the snide parting remarks. The universe really knew how to douse her with cold water right before she was about to throw caution to the wind. The quick incident had reminded her that Tyrone was a hit-it-and-quit-it type of guy and she was no longer playing sexual pit stop for a man.

Sheri spotted Kiera and her eyes widened. "Oh, my bad. I thought everyone was gone."

Sheri was slim, with dark skin and big bright eyes. The volunteer T-shirt, which was baggy on everyone else, clung to her full breasts, and her long dark hair was pulled back in a ponytail. She reminded Kiera of a model, and she didn't miss that Sheri's skin was radiant and smooth without makeup.

"I'm just finishing up." Kiera turned back and gave a brief glance at her reflection in the mirror. Her makeup was still perfect and flawless. Though, she didn't want to think too hard about why she cared.

Sheri nodded. "Cool. I just need to check the room before the next panelist comes in. The producer with your show left something in here." She crossed the room and picked up a black bag.

"So, you're from here?" Kiera asked as Sheri headed toward the door.

She stopped then nodded. "I grew up in Sunshine Beach, but I've only been back in town for about three or four years. My mom was sick, and I came back."

"Then you grew up with the Livingston brothers?" Why was she asking? She wasn't supposed to care.

Sheri faced her and watched Kiera intently. "I did. Dion and Wesley are great guys. I have no problem with them."

The unspoken words were clear and her eyes didn't leave Kiera's. She *did* had a problem with Tyrone. Kiera wanted to ask. Wanted to find out what happened, but that was going too far. She wasn't his real girlfriend. She wasn't here to find out about the women he dated because she wasn't dating him for real.

"It's good to hear that," Kiera said.

Sheri's eyes narrowed slightly as if she was trying to figure out Kiera. After a second, she shook her head and pointed to the door. "Well, I need to get this to your producer."

Kiera closed her makeup bag and held out a hand. "I can take it. I'm going to that panel, anyway."

She told herself she was only doing this because Tyrone seemed uncomfortable when he'd seen Sheri before. She was only trying to make things easier before they had their first panel. Not that she didn't want this beautiful woman from his past to have a reason to be in close contact with him.

"Sure, if you want to." She handed the bag to Kiera. "Enjoy the panel."

Kiera took the bag, then nodded and watched Sheri walk out. She quickly packed up her stuff then went into the room where Tyron and his brothers would answer questions about their show. She took the bag to Tiana, gave the brothers a thumbs-up and then sat in the front row next to Vanessa and Cierra, who'd both come to support their men.

The guys did great. They answered the questions about the show, paranormal investigations and why they loved what they do. The entire time they were charming, funny and serious about their devotion to their work. Kiera was swept into the discussion and even more intrigued by her fake boyfriend. After the panel, she stood to the side and watched as attendees came over for selfies and autographs.

She glanced around the room and caught Sheri's eye. Sheri looked from Kiera toward Tyrone. Kiera followed her gaze to where Tyrone was standing with his arm wrapped around a female fan. He held out the woman's phone so they could take a selfie. She didn't miss the way the woman wrapped her arms tightly around his waist, or the way she pressed her body close to his.

A quick scan of Dion and Wes proved they were good about keeping an adequate amount of space between them and any of the fans they took pictures with. Her eyes drifted back to Sheri. Sheri gave her a better-you-than-me smirk, before walking out of the room.

Kiera turned back to Tyrone. He'd peeled the eager fan from his side and all three brothers were taking a picture with another fan. Kiera kept the smile on her face. Pretended as if she'd missed the clingy fan and turned to talk to Vanessa and Cierra about how great the panel had gone. She pushed aside Sheri's smirk and the queasy feeling in her stomach. Tyrone wasn't her real boyfriend. Jealousy had no place in this arrangement. She didn't care about his relationship with Sheri or any other woman as long as he wasn't sleeping with anyone else while they did this. No matter how much she repeated the thought, she couldn't let go of her curiosity.

Dion and Vanessa went back to Charlotte after the convention so they could both get back to work before filming picked up later in the week. Kiera could have returned to Atlanta and scheduled a few makeup jobs over the week, but one phone call with her mom revealed that her brother had indeed spilled the beans. Her mother made it very clear that as soon as Kiera returned home, she wanted her to come over and tell everything about her new boyfriend and to schedule a date for when they both could come over for dinner. Her mom loved the *Haunted Homeboys* show and her dad had probably told half the neighborhood about Kiera's new boyfriend.

Going home meant lying to her parents' faces, and she wasn't ready for that. It was much easier to feign new-relationship bliss over the phone. Therefore, she decided to stay in Sunshine Beach until filming started. Without Dion and Vanessa there, she was able to move into the third bedroom. The new sleeping arrangement made keeping their fake relationship platonic a whole lot easier.

The morning after the convention, she sat at the kitchen table, drinking coffee and checking her emails on her cell phone. Two minutes in and she wondered if picking up a few extra jobs might have been worth facing her parents. Her in-box was full of reminders about a new statement for another bill waiting for her review. She'd thought going paperless on some bills would make her feel less crappy about her debt; instead, having an email in-box full of statements was just as bad as having her regular mailbox full.

Tyrone came downstairs as she went through the process of setting up online payments. No automatic drafts for her. Her accounts required careful watching and strategic placement of what amount of money went where, so she could go from month to month without a major mishap.

"Hey, what are you up to?" Tyrone asked. He went to the pantry and pulled out a box of Cap'n Crunch cereal.

"Paying bills," she said, frowning at her phone.

"Ugh, a necessary evil." He put the cereal and a bowl on the table before getting milk out of the fridge.

"Tell me about it," she mumbled. She hit "pay now" and visualized her bank account draining from the payments.

"That bad?" Tyrone asked after sitting down next to her.

She sighed and put down her phone. "Kind of. I broke my ankle about a year and a half ago and the medical bills piled up. I couldn't work while I healed and had physical therapy afterward. Add the medical bills to the student loans and trying to keep a decent apartment in the Paces area, and yeah…it's bad."

"Sorry," he said sounding genuinely empathetic to her situation.

"Don't be. Your lie is actually helping me out." He'd just stuffed a spoonful of cereal into his mouth and raised his eyebrows in curiosity. "Dating you got me the steady paycheck on your show. I'm making enough money to start putting a dent in the debt."

He swallowed and wiped his mouth. "Really?"

"Yep, so thank you for that."

He saluted her with the spoon. "You're welcome."

She grinned and rested her forearms on the table. "Plus, the publicity will hopefully boost interest in my online channel about makeup and get me more clients. I can't forget why I went along with this in the first place."

His eyebrows drew together, but he had a mouth full of cereal and didn't respond. Kiera glanced at her phone and closed her bank's app. They both needed the reminder. This was a transactional relationship they were in. That's all.

"What about you?" she asked.

He swallowed. "What about me?"

"Why were you so eager for the second season? Are you climbing out of student-loan debt like I am?"

Tyrone shook his head. "Not really. When Dion dropped out of school to keep us together, he used most of the money from our parents' life insurance to pay off the house. The rest he saved for me and Wesley to use for college. I didn't get any debt."

"I'd say you were lucky, but I'm pretty sure you'd rather have had your parents."

The corner of his mouth lifted in a sad smile and he poked at the cereal in the bowl. "I would, but I still appreciate what Dion did for us."

"Okay, so it's not money. But I think it's more than just not wanting to mess up a second season."

He chewed and considered her words. After he

swallowed, he shrugged and met her eye. "I love doing this. Dion and Wes weren't originally on board with doing a show. Yeah, we had fun investigating ghosts, but this was never their passion. Dion likes helping people, but he's too structured to trust his retirement plans on a successful television show. Wes is an architect and creating things is his thing. They both kept their jobs and take out the time to film the show. If it fails, they're good."

"But you're not?"

He shrugged. "It's not the same. I'm sure I could go back to the station or somewhere else, but I always dreamed big. I wanted something more than the regular day-to-day, nine-to-five job. If the show fails… I fail."

"You're not a failure if the show fails. There are so many things that go into making a show successful. Things out of your control. You're smart and creative enough to land somewhere else even if the show is canceled."

"Maybe so, but I also love investigating ghosts. This is like my dream job. My brothers were fascinated by ghosts after my grandmother told us stories and stuff, but I was the one who first convinced them to figure out if the old house on the edge of town was really haunted."

"How did you do that?"

"By getting them to spend the night there," he said

easily, as if spending the night in a haunted house was as easy as riding a tricycle.

She playfully slapped his shoulder. "What? Why would you do that?"

He laughed. "I don't know. Now I realize it might not have been my best idea, but I was fascinated. Life after death. Souls and spirits. I wanted to know why some people stick around and the reasons they do. So do my brothers. It didn't take much to get them to say yes to staying in that old house."

She propped an elbow on the table and then rested her chin in her hand. "I get it. It's not just having a show, it's having a show doing what you love. That's why you did this."

"I always wanted to know more. Now, I get paid to investigate and find out what I can about the other side. Where else will I get paid to do this?"

With her head tilted to the side, she watched him. Just like listening to him on the panel the day before, she had a greater appreciation for him and the work he did. "I think it's pretty cool."

He gave her a quizzical look. "You do? I either get people who are frightened or think I'm bonkers for trying to find ghosts."

"I get people who think I'm being silly for wanting to play in makeup all day. They don't understand that I don't see makeup as just a way to indulge in some superficial need. When you feel good about yourself, then you're more confident. It takes different things to make people feel confident and beautiful. Makeup can be one person's armor before they go out and face the world."

He stopped stirring his cereal and stared intently at her. "Do you view it as your armor?"

"It gives me confidence, so in a way, I guess, yes."

"What would you do if you didn't have makeup?"

She didn't think she'd be as lost and self-conscious as she'd been when she was younger. She definitely wouldn't accept any insults or sly comments about her looks as she'd once done. She was stronger now, her self-confidence better, but she also didn't want to admit that the idea of letting go of the one thing that made her feel completely in control was scary.

"I don't know. What would you do if you weren't investigating ghosts?" she asked back.

He looked to the ceiling and pursed his lips. "Hmm... I'd still be working at the radio station, which wouldn't be bad because I enjoyed working there. I'd still be interested and want to know more, but I know I'd be looking for a way to find happiness in something around me."

"You weren't happy before the show?"

"I wasn't unhappy, more like I was frustrated. Everyone in this town kept comparing me to Dion and Wes. All I heard after my parents died was how I needed to grow up, go to college, get married and have babies. After I grew up, all I got was when am I going to settle down, quit playing around and planning parties. I just want to do what I love and not be questioned or told I should be doing something else. I'm all about doing what I want, when I want, without answering to anyone."

Which explained why he was so against commitment. Tyrone was a live-life-on-his-own-terms kind of person. Begging him to do one thing would only make him push away. She'd be smart to remember that before she started asking that he treat her as if she was his real girlfriend.

His whiskey-brown eyes met hers. "What about you? What makes you happy?"

After his declaration, she didn't want to admit that one day she would like to settle down. Live a quiet, predictable life. Have kids and buy a cute house in a nice subdivision. Not that she planned to give up her career or her dreams of being a well-known makeup artist, but having one didn't mean she couldn't have the other.

"Making money," she said with a smile. That part was true and he already knew it.

Tyrone laughed. "Then let's make as much as we can, sweetheart."

She cringed. "I don't like that one either, honeybun."

He scrunched up his nose and shook his head. Kiera laughed and got up to make more coffee. Yeah, she was here to make money. Tyrone would never be the man in her suburban-life fantasy.

Chapter Eleven

Kiera leaned forward in the portable folding chair to peer at the video of Tyrone and his brothers. They were investigating the haunting of an abandoned theater in Georgetown, South Carolina. The sun was down, and darkness blanketed the sky, yet Kiera and Tiana were still sitting beneath the tent set up for the crew in the vacant lot across the street. Although she'd watched their show before, she was riveted. Previously she'd wondered how much was staged for the show and how much was really ghosts. Today, she'd gotten her answer. There were no signs of staging, no extra lights or someone hiding behind a door making knocking sounds. Everything they'd discovered seemed real.

Not only was she fascinated by what they did, but

she was also drawn in as she watched Tyrone. His excitement and enthusiasm were evident in the way his eyes lit up whenever their spirit box, the machine they used to communicate with the ghosts, buzzed and crackled. With each discovery, the bounce in his step increased. He reminded her of someone who'd struck continuous jackpots. He was so excited, he also wanted to charge ahead regardless of the consequences.

"Are they really going down there?" Tiana asked.

Her production assistant, Haley, slowly nodded her head. "I think they are."

Tiana shook her head. "The plan wasn't to go down there. I thought there were structural issues or something." She pointed at one of the two monitors on the table. "Dion looks a little concerned. Make sure we get a close-up shot of that."

Haley relayed the request through her walkie-talkie to Dorian, the cameraman, who would hear it on an earpiece so it wouldn't be caught by his camera. Kiera frowned at the screen and shook her head. The brothers were debating whether to go into the basement of the theater. Wesley said he had a bad feeling about going down, which, of course, only made Tyrone want to go even more and find out what was going on down there. Tiana's storyline for the night's filming was to focus on the theater's upstairs and old offices. During the investigation, the discovery that there may be more activity in the basement made Tyrone want to go off script, while Dion wasn't budging on the stance that they stay away from the restricted area.

"Let's take a break and talk it out before we make a decision," Tiana said.

Kiera agreed and let out a breath when Tiana called "cut." She grabbed her makeup bag, tissues and a few brushes, and followed Tiana across the street to where the brothers were exiting the theater. They really didn't need her to be on set to do their makeup, but she was there to provide behind-the-scenes shots of her and Tyrone. Kiera also took a few selfies with Tyrone and his brothers during breaks that she'd post on social media later.

They'd barely gotten out of the door before Tyrone asked irritably, "Why did we stop? Things were just getting good."

Kiera hurried over to him and pulled out a napkin to wipe the sweat on this brow. It was warm for late September and the boarded windows made the air inside the theater stifling.

Tiana crossed her arms. "Going into the basement wasn't a part of today's plan. How about we make sure everyone is good before you go bebopping down the stairs?"

"I'm more than good," Tyrone said. "We're close to finding out what happened here. We can't not go down there."

"But we can't just be reckless, either," Dion said. "We aren't the only ones going down."

Tyrone's head jerked toward his brother. Kiera put her hand on his chin and turned him back to her. When he frowned, she shook her head. "Listen to your brother."

"What?"

"He's not going against you. He wants to make sure everyone is safe, but you're ready to run downstairs without knowing what's down there. Let them check with the property owner and be sure the basement is okay to enter."

"But—"

She dabbed her brush against his temples to quiet him. "But nothing. Better safe than sorry. Please, do this without hurting yourself or anyone else."

He looked ready to argue, but she pursed her lips and stared back. After a few seconds, his shoulders relaxed and he sighed. "Fine."

Tiana's eyes widened. "Damn, Kiera, I wish you were dating him last year."

Kiera suppressed a chuckle and Tyrone frowned. He didn't say anything else as Tiana walked away to talk to the property owner about what to expect in the basement.

"You like that, huh?" Tyrone asked, keeping his voice down.

Kiera finished blotting his face and smirked. "Like what?"

"Getting praised for keeping the hotheaded Tyrone Livingston under control."

"You're not hotheaded, you're enthusiastic. That's clear to me and everyone else down here. That doesn't mean you have to argue because your brother wants to be cautious before you go into a new space."

"Dion's always been too cautious," he grumbled.

Kiera used a blotter to reduce the shine across his forehead and nose. "And maybe you've always been a little reckless."

"Says who?"

She leaned in and lowered her voice. "Can I remind you why I'm here?"

The defensive look in his eyes evaporated and the corner of his mouth rose in a half smile. "You know how to hit hard, don't you?"

"Nah, but I do know how to reason." She patted his cheek. "This will take a few minutes and you can get right back to seeing what that ghost wants y'all to see."

His eyes lit up again. "You notice that he's trying to show us something."

She grinned and dropped her hand from his cheek to his chest. "You're cute when you're excited."

He stepped closer, his eyes turning playful. "Oh, really? How cute?"

Cute enough to make her want to lean up on her toes and kiss him. He'd been good as they'd lived together for the past few days before filming. He'd kept his distance, hadn't brought up them sleeping together and respected her wishes to keep their relationship platonic, which she appreciated. She hadn't asked him about his relationship with Sheri or any other women he'd dated, but that didn't mean she'd forgotten them.

"Alright you two. Stop it," Dion's said. He and Wesley walked over. "We aren't going to make it through the season if you're going to be making love with your eyes every time you're together."

Tyrone grinned. "I can't help it if she thinks I'm irresistible."

Kiera poked his shoulder. "I said you were cute. Not irresistible."

Wesley chuckled. "Your eyes said irresistible."

Kiera's cheeks flamed but before she could say more Tiana was back. "The owner says it's okay to go in the basement, but there may be standing water. The basement floods and there was rain a few days ago. We're going to check for water and if it's dry you can do down."

Tyrone rubbed his hands together. "Bet, let's go."

The brothers nodded and headed that way. Tyrone turned around and ran back to her. She frowned but he shook his head. "Nothing's wrong, but thank you."

"For what?"

He rubbed the back of his head. "You're right, I get excited and would have rushed down there without checking first. Thanks for keeping me from snapping at my brother for no reason."

"That's what girlfriends do, right?"

"You keep saying that and I'll make you my girlfriend forever."

Despite the jolt to her pulse, she took his words with a grain of salt. Tyrone was flirting with her as he always flirted. Playing the part of loving boyfriend for the dozens of people watching them. Even now, she could see Dorian pointing the camera in their direction.

"Who says I'll have you?"

He grinned his heart-stopping grin. "Quit playing. I'm respecting your wishes, but that doesn't mean I'm not still waiting." He leaned in to whisper in her ear. "I meant what I said about waiting for you to be okay with us making some parts of this real. It's on you, Kiera. When you want me, you can have me."

He pulled back, the sexy smirk still on his face, then turned and jogged to catch up with his brothers. Kiera watched him go with wide eyes and a pounding heart. Her eyes narrowed and she wagged a finger in the direction he'd taken off.

"Oh, you're good," she murmured. She placed a hand on her chest. Her heart pumped fast against her palm. Her brain knew he was teasing her, but her heart, her body, didn't care that this was just for show. Nor did either recognize that believing anything Tyrone said would only lead to heartbreak later.

He turned to look at her over his shoulder. He winked and smiled. Kiera smiled back then whispered to herself, "But, boy, would it be fun just to go along for the ride."

Tyrone watched Kiera's face as they got out of his car. When her eyes widened, and she looked at him with an are-you-serious expression, he smiled. "Why are you looking like that?"

"This is the house?" She pointed at the dilapidated two-story structure in front of them.

Tyrone laughed, closed the space between them and wrapped his arm around her shoulder. He turned her toward the house but at an angle so Dorian could get a good shot of them together. Tiana stood behind Dorian. The rest of the crew wasn't there because this was a quick look at Tyrone and his relationship with Kiera. A day where he showed her around his hometown and told stories about his past.

"This is the house," he said.

"You convinced your brothers to spend the night... here?"

"It wasn't this bad back when we spent the night," he said.

"Are you sure, because this house looks as if it was ready to fall down two decades ago," she said.

Green mold and overgrown vines covered the outside of the dilapidated structure that may have once been white but now looked gray. The stairs lead-ing up to the house had rotted and all the windows were broken.

Tyrone dropped his arm and gave her a side-eye. She just shrugged. "I mean, it does."

Shaking his head, he stood behind her, put his hands on her shoulders and focused on the house. Again, in a position that gave the camera a good angle. If they were going to follow him and Kiera around, then he was going to get the most out of things. Kiera agreed that today they needed to play up the new-couple-in-love angle while Dorian and Tiana followed them around.

So far, they'd gotten shots of the two of them in his family home eating breakfast and discussing the schedule, video of him on the phone with Dion planning for a dinner between the brothers and their significant others, and now the house where he and his brothers had done their first investigation as inquisitive teens.

"I'm serious. It wasn't this bad when we stayed the night."

Kiera turned her head and looked at him over her shoulder. "Do you still go in there and check things out?" Kiera asked.

When she looked at him, with her skin glowing in the sunlight and whatever gloss she'd put on her lips making them appear even more plump and enticing, all he wanted to do was turn her in his arms and cover her mouth with his. Tiana and Dorian would love it, but Kiera wouldn't. Pretending to be a couple was awkward enough. He wasn't going to push her into his bed. That didn't mean he wouldn't give gentle nudges for her to give in to the desire he often saw swimming in her brown eyes.

He brushed his fingers across her cheek to get the hair out of her eyes. She'd removed the longer extensions and her short hair was styled with just an extra bit of hair in the front. Her lips parted with his touch and her breathing hitched.

"Nah, I don't go inside anymore. We know the story behind the spirits haunting the place. I haven't been out here since…"

She quickly turned back to look at the house. "Since when?"

He wanted to turn her back around so he could see that look on her face. The look that said she wanted him just like he wanted her. He wanted to bask in and savor that look. Instead he was a good boy and got back to the house.

"Since I had to pick up Vanessa's car. She got stuck out here and Dion had to come rescue her."

Kiera spun back around to stare at him, wide-eyed. "Say what now?"

He shook his head and laughed. "Not my story to tell." He looked at Tiara and Dorian. "But be sure to ask Dion and Vanessa about it." He leaned in and whispered in her ear, "I'll tell you later."

Kiera nodded and laughed. "Oh, I'm going to ask about it later."

Tiana wrote a note in the notebook in her hand. "I'll be sure to bring that up. Do you want to go in the house?"

Tyrone shook his head. "No need. The place is pretty dilapidated now. I wouldn't want anyone to get hurt."

Tiana gave him an appreciative look before glancing at Kiera with what he could only call admiration. "Let's get some shots of you two walking around the house," she said. "Maybe tell her the history of the haunting. Be sure you're holding hands and being really touchy-feely and stuff. The viewers love to see the couples on our shows showing affection. That's not a problem, is it?"

Tyrone looked to Kiera first. She'd been okay with everything they'd asked for them to do as a couple, but he still deferred to her before agreeing. She was doing him a favor, after all. As eager as he was, having Kiera come to him of her own will without any pressure on his part would be worth every restless night and unanswered fantasy.

"It's good with me," she said.

He nodded then gave Tiana a thumbs-up. "We've got it."

He held out his hand and Kiera put hers in his. He like that, too. He liked a lot about their relationship. Kiera was so chill. She didn't just make assumptions or label him as a hothead or difficult. She understood he was passionate about what he did and driven. He liked the way she both supported him and calmed him. He liked holding her hand and the way she'd lean into him when they walked.

He'd seen too many relationships where there was to much drama, and couples having to work hard to prove to the other person how much they cared. Yeah, his brothers had found happiness, but they'd gone through their share of bad relationships before finding the women who worked for them. Then he'd also wondered how anyone would be happy with having sex with just one person for an extended period of time. But he hadn't even slept with Kiera and there was no other woman he wanted right now. He hated to admit it, but Kiera was making him rethink his stance on long-term relationships.

They walked around the exterior of the house. Tyrone gave background info on the doctor who'd lived there and was acquitted of killing his wife, only later, according to legend, to be killed by his wife's ghost seeking revenge on him and his mistress. Kiera seemed enthralled by the story, asking questions and showing interest in learning more about how he and his brothers searched historical records to learn as much as they could about the lives of the people haunting the places they investigated.

On the way back toward the front of the house, Kiera tripped over an exposed root of one of the old maple trees. Tyrone immediately reached out and placed one arm around her wrist to keep her from falling.

"Hold that position," Tiana called out before Tyrone could straighten.

He froze in the awkward position with his arm around her waist. Kiera held herself stiff even though by now he assumed she was able to get her balance.

Tiana held out her hands and watched them through the frame of her fingers. "Now, pull her back and into your arms."

"What?" Tyrone said.

"Pull her back and then wrap your other arm around her waist. It'll be like in one of those romantic movies or something. We'll slow it down for effect. Then stare into each other's eyes. Let the viewers see how much you two care about each other."

Kiera glanced up at him and nodded. That was all he needed. Once Dorian was in place, he pulled her up and spun her until she faced him. Her hands landed on his chest, while his rested along the curve of her hips. He didn't have to pretend to stare because he was riveted by the look in her eyes: playful and seductive. A small smile hovered over her full lips at the extra ness of the situation. She thought this was just as over-the-top as he did. Their lips trembled from suppressed laughter, but when her breasts rubbed against his chest, he forgot about the camera.

The smile slowly faded from his face as he stared at the beautiful woman in his arms.

Kiera's hands slid up his chest to rest on his shoulders. After a heartbeat, she leaned up on her toes and pressed a kiss to the corner of his mouth. "Thank you, baby." Exaggerated sweetness filled her voice as she played up the situation.

His stomach clenched and his heart lurched. He didn't know if it was the sunshine, that gloss on her lips, or the need pumping through his veins, but Tyrone indulged his instincts and kissed her. Her lips parted with a soft gasp a half second before her body softened against him. Angels sang in his head when she didn't pull away. His tongue glided across her full lower lip and damn, if that gloss didn't taste like strawberries. Groaning, he pulled her closer to his body. He wanted to kiss her forever. To drown in the softness of her lips before losing himself in the sweet heat of her. He wanted this woman more than he'd craved anyone else and the thought scared the crap out of him.

He was about to be lost. He knew it. He'd never been lost in a woman before and he damn sure didn't want to do it here. Not because he was afraid of losing himself in her. Oh, no, he was going to enjoy the hell out of indulging in every fantasy he had with Kiera. He did not want to lose himself in front of a broken-down haunted house and a camera that would take this moment and cheapen it for ratings.

He pulled back slowly. Kiera stared back at him with dazed eyes. His lips lifted in a slow smile. "You good?"

She nodded slowly. "Very good."

His heart soared. Tiana said something about keeping things PG, but Tyrone didn't care. Judging by the yearning in Kiera's eyes, she was ready to admit the chemistry between them wasn't worth ignoring for much longer.

Chapter Twelve

Their final stop was at a local diner downtown. Everyone was hungry and Tyrone insisted they visit a local business not only to get good shots of him showing Kiera the town, but also to bring recognition to a place he enjoyed visiting. The soul-food restaurant, Auntie's, had opened ten years ago and was one of the most popular places downtown to get a full meal at a reasonable price.

They walked in and Tyrone immediately recognized several of the people sitting around the tables or waiting for food near the takeout counter in the back. The excitement in the place increased when they entered with the camera. Tyrone looked over at Tiana and Dorian. "Let me check with Auntie to be sure she's okay with us filming."

Tiana nodded then rubbed her stomach. "Sounds good, but even if she's not, I'm ordering. The food smells delicious."

"It is delicious. I'll be right back." He headed toward the counter in the back to talk to Auntie, the owner. On the way he caught the eye of a person in the back booth and cringed. Li'l Bit and Cora were sitting together with a group of their friends.

Tyrone suppressed a groan when Cora's eyes narrowed on him. He looked away, then hurried over to the counter and called for Auntie. They just needed to order and get out of there. Hopefully, they could do that without having to interact with Sheri or her cousin.

Auntie came from the back. "Tyrone! What are you doing here with that camera?" Auntie was in her late fifties, with a short, faded afro and a wide smile with a cute gap between her two front teeth. A pair of jeans hugged her ample hips and she was wearing a pink shirt with the word *Auntie's* across the front.

Tyrone leaned down and gave her a hug. "We're just ordering to go. I hope you don't mind if we get a few shots of your place for the show?"

Auntie immediately patted her head. "Mind! Boy, you know I don't mind. Be sure to get a good shot of the sign out front and the people in here enjoying the food. Is this really going to be on your show?"

Tyrone nodded. "Yes, ma'am."

Auntie's grin widened. "Tyrone Livingston, you're alright with me."

Tyrone laughed and waved over Kiera, Tiana and Dorian. He made the introductions and Tiana immediately went into production mode and talked about the shots she'd like to get inside the restaurant and of Auntie.

Tyrone noticed the moment when Kiera spotted Sheri and Cora. She'd been glancing around at the various pictures on the walls and stiffened when she looked in the back corner. He placed his hand on the small of her back and leaned in.

"It's been a long day. Are you good with getting the food to go?"

"Yeah, I think that would be for the best."

He told Auntie and Tiana, and although they groaned, Tiana and Dorian also had long days and were scheduled to film Wes with Cierra and her daughter later that evening.

Dorian gave Tyrone a sly look. "You say you're tired, but I saw that kiss. You two are just ready to get back home and ditch us."

Kiera popped him across the shoulder and laughed. Tiana and Auntie joined in. Tyrone didn't miss the grunt from the back corner. Probably Cora—Sheri just glared at him most of the time.

They placed their to-go orders while Dorian filmed them ordering and talking to Auntie. When Dorian asked if it was okay to get a few shots of some of the unique photos and posters on the wall, Auntie quickly agreed.

The door to the restaurant opened and Vanessa's grandmother, Mrs. Montgomery, came in. She saw Tyrone and immediately waved. Short and plump, with tawny brown skin and laugh lines around her eyes and mouth, Arletha Montgomery pulled him into a warm welcoming hug.

"Look at you. Got the camera crew and everything," she said when she pulled back. "You boys are really going to make our town famous."

"I don't know about all that," he said with a shy smile. "Mrs. Montgomery, this is Kiera Cox."

Kiera reached over and took her hand. "It's nice to meet you."

"Oh, it's definitely nice to meet you. Are you the girlfriend?"

Kiera nodded. "Yes, ma'am, I am."

Mrs. Montgomery nodded her approval. "I just love it. The baby Livingston brother finally found someone to make him happy. I'm glad to see it." She looked at Tyrone and grinned. "You boys deserve love and happiness."

The sound of a snort came from behind them. They all turned to see Cora standing there with a hand on her hip. She eyed Tyrone as if he was a disease. "Excuse me, but I need to pay my bill."

Mrs. Montgomery frowned. "Now, Cora, why are you acting like that?"

"I'm sorry, Mrs. Montgomery, but I just can't stand the way everyone is fawning over Tyrone when we all know he did my cousin wrong."

Mrs. Montgomery pointed a finger. "That's between Tyrone and Li'l Bit. Did he do you wrong?"

Cora dropped her eyes. "No, ma'am."

"Then mind your business. Now go on and pay your bill."

Cora nodded; she threw one last ugly glance at Tyrone before going to the counter. So many eyes in the restaurant were now on them. He almost kissed Auntie when she brought out their to-go plates. He grabbed the food in one hand and Kiera's hand in the other.

"We'll see you, Mrs. Montgomery. Thanks so much, Auntie"

Mrs. Montgomery gave him a knowing smile. "See you later, baby. Nice to meet you, Kiera."

"Nice to meet you, too." Kiera's voice was polite, but the earlier cheerfulness was gone.

He headed toward the door and once they were outside, Tiana asked Kiera, "How does it feel to have people question Tyrone's past in front of you?"

Tyrone glared at Tiana. He thought they were cool, but, of course, she was a reality-show producer first and foremost. Any hint of potential drama for a future episode and she'd find a way to work this into the season.

Kiera stiffened, then shrugged and let her shoulders relaxed. "I knew who he was before we started dating. We've talked about things, and I trust him. That's all that matters now."

Tiana raised an eyebrow. "Are you sure?"

Kiera squeezed his hand and smiled at him. "I'm sure. I don't care about his past. I only care about how he treats me."

A vise of emotion squeezed Tyrone's heart. Kiera was absolutely the most perfect girlfriend ever.

Chapter Thirteen

As soon as they were behind the closed doors of Tyrone's place with Tiana and Dorian gone after they'd eaten, and the threat of being overheard was gone, Kiera turned on Tyrone. "Tell me what happened."

He'd plopped down on the couch in the family room and was reaching for the remote. "What happened?"

"With that girl Sheri and her cousin."

He left the remote on the coffee table and leaned back into the cushions of the sofa. He sighed and rubbed his face. "I thought you didn't care."

Kiera sat on the edge of the sectional farthest away from him. She'd pretended not to care to avoid unnecessary drama. Now the drama was coming to her.

"That was then, but if she's going to approach us

when the cameras are around that means I'm going to be asked about your past again. If I'm going to be 'standing by my man—'" she made air quotes with her fingers "—then I need to know if you're worth standing by."

He scowled, but Kiera didn't break eye contact. Tyrone was a flirt and obviously didn't want a long-term relationship, but he hadn't given her any indication that he was a dog. The way he treated her and respected her boundaries had lured her into believing he was a nice guy. Today the truth had been shoved in her face again. Just because he wasn't terrible to her didn't mean he hadn't been terrible to other women. If he'd done something awful to Sheri then she wouldn't be able to pretend to be his girlfriend no matter the consequences.

"Li'l Bit was mad, but her cousin has always carried a grudge."

"Looks like she's carrying a pretty big grudge. Is what happened really that small or are you being overly dismissive?"

Tyrone sat up straight and met her eye. "I'm not that type of guy. You want to know what happened, then I'll tell you."

She crossed her arms and settled more comfortably on the sectional. "Go on."

Tyrone took a long breath before talking. "I've known Li'l Bit—Sheri—for most of my life. We went to middle and high school together and we were always cool with each other. She's cool with my brothers, too. Everyone likes her because she's laid-back and easy to get along with. After my parents died, her family stepped in and helped out, and we hooked up once after graduation."

Kiera's eyebrows drew together. "She's mad because you hooked up once after high school?"

Tyrone shook his head. "Nah, I'm just giving you background. I went to college, so did she, and that was it. I came back home to work at the radio station, and she was living in Columbia, I think. Her mom got sick, and she moved back home. We ran into each other one night, talked about that one time we hooked up in high school. One thing led to another and…"

"You slept together."

He nodded. "We did. The next morning, I told her that I wasn't looking for anything serious, and she said the same. We both agreed it shouldn't happen again, but when she came by my place a few nights later…" He shrugged. "I didn't say no."

Of course, he didn't. "How long did this go on?"

"Maybe about a month or two. It was just hookups. Late-night texts to see if the other was free."

"What happened?"

He met her eyes. "I met someone else at a party. I knew I needed to stop what I was doing with Li'l Bit before I started with another person. I don't like confusion or playing around with people's emotions. Unless they agreed, sleeping with more than one woman is a recipe for disaster. I talked to Sheri. I told her I thought we should stop, and she agreed. Then she saw me out with the other woman a few weeks later, called me later that night and cursed me out, and then keyed my car. It's been weird and awkward ever since."

"Did you really not sleep with that other woman while seeing Sheri?"

Kiera watched for any signs that he was lying. She wasn't a mind reader, but she was a pretty good judge of knowing when someone lied to her. It's how she'd known it was time to end things with her ex, Mike. Their on-again, off-again relationship hadn't been one she expected to turn into a happily-ever-after, but when she'd caught him lying about seeing someone else when they were back on, she'd realized a small part of her had expected a future with him. Otherwise, why would she have still been putting so much effort into a relationship with a man who couldn't even commit to her for the two to three months they'd decided to be back together?

Tyrone shook his head. "I don't play around like that. Even after I found out Sheri keyed my car and the cops asked if I wanted to press charges, I said no because I wasn't trying to drag things out like that. I tried talking to her after and she said she just wanted to move on."

"Have you apologized to her?"

He blinked, then frowned. "For what? I was upfront

from the start, I broke things off before moving on and I got my car keyed. What do I need to apologize for?"

Kiera shrugged. "Emotions are funny. I get that you two were only hooking up and not technically dating, but you did so for over a month. Let me guess—in that time you both said you were going to stop but never did."

He opened his mouth as if to argue, then sighed. "Yeah a few times."

"Maybe she didn't think the last time you said it was any different than before. Then seeing you with someone else was a shock. I'm not saying keying your car was right, but people lash out when hurt and angry."

"We both said we would move on." Tyrone sounded confused. As if the agreement was enough to keep out emotions and hurt feelings.

"Well, obviously she hasn't. She's still upset, and her cousin is, too. Did you ever wonder if the rumors about you started with her?"

He grimaced. "I did, but I'd also hoped she wouldn't go that far."

"Maybe she didn't, but it's probably a good idea to clear the air. Especially since this season is focused around your family and hometown. Is this everything? There's nothing else I need to know?"

He sat up straight and placed a hand over his heart. "That's everything. I try to be upfront and honest because I don't want to cause any drama. Do you believe me?"

She stared into his eyes and considered what he'd said. His gaze didn't waver and he didn't break eye contact. She trusted his words, but that didn't make hearing them any easier. She wasn't jealous of his relationship with Li'l Bit. He was a grown man and was bound to have previous relationships, some of them messy. Her relationship with Mike had been messy and unfulfilling. She'd caught him in the lie and wanted to throw a brick through his window. If she'd run in to him with the woman shortly after they'd broken up, she might have done so.

Knowing this did one thing for her. It proved her decision to keep her relationship with Tyrone platonic was the right one. She liked him already. Sleeping with him would make it harder to keep her emotions out of things. This was a fake relationship to benefit them both. If she forgot that, she'd end up heartbroken, potentially without a job and still in debt.

"Kiera?" he asked.

She gave him a tight smile and nodded. "I believe you."

He didn't relax or appear relieved. He leaned forward and placed his elbows on his knees. "Are we still good?"

"We are. It's like I told you before. We're doing this to help each other out. I'm not your real girlfriend, so I'm not upset about your past." He scowled and opened his mouth to say something but she cut in. "It's been a long day. I'm going to go up to rest for a little bit."

She stood and walked toward the door. A few seconds later Tyrone's hand closed around hers. She turned to face him. He was standing so close their chests almost touched.

The light hit his eyes, lightening the brown and making the fire of his frustration, and something else she couldn't name, bright in his gaze. "Do you really not care?"

His grip of her arm was light. She could break away if she wanted, but she didn't break away. Even after their talk and knowing Tyrone wasn't the man for her, she still craved his touch.

"I care about getting through this without any problems. We're doing this for a reason, remember?" Her voice was soft but thankfully strong.

He took a half step closer. His chest brushed her breasts. His eyes searched hers. For what, she didn't know. "Is that it? You don't feel anything else?"

The heat of his body caressed hers. The fire in his gaze burned her soul. Kiera's skin prickled. She swallowed hard, breaking eye contact first. Her gaze dropped to his lips. The memory of the kiss from earlier consumed her. She'd been willing to forget this was all for show when he'd kissed her. She'd been swept up in the fantasy and Tyrone was all too good at playing the devoted, loving boyfriend. But one day the fantasy would end. Someone else would come along for him and she'd still be wearing the tinted, rose-colored glasses, believing he was her happily-ever-after.

Kiera stepped back. His fingers dropped from her arm. When she met his eyes again, she ignored the longing reflected there. He longed for something she couldn't afford to give. "That's all I can feel. I don't want to be the next woman keying your car."

Chapter Fourteen

Tyrone watched Kiera standing across the road laughing with other members of the crew while he and his brothers went over the details of the upcoming investigation. They were investigating a suspected angry spirit in a home outside Wilmington, North Carolina. The home belonged to a married couple with two young kids, who'd recently moved in. They were about to have the initial on-camera interview with the family about what they'd experienced before he and his brothers spent the night to observe for themselves. The next day, they'd film the three of them researching the history of the property and the home.

He'd looked forward to this investigation from the moment he'd learned about it, yet he couldn't focus on anything except Kiera. Since they'd talked about his relationship with Sheri, she'd been the same but different. They still got along, were still able to laugh and joke with each other, and pretend to be a loving couple for the cameras. Yet, he could tell she was holding back a part of herself. The flirtatious look in her eyes had dimmed and she pulled back when she once would've leaned in.

He should be okay with that. They weren't really together. He didn't want to be in another situation similar to the one with Sheri. Clearly, she didn't, either. Keeping things as they were was the smart thing to do. He knew that, so why did he feel as if it was all so wrong?

Someone tapped him on the shoulder. "Tyrone, you listening?"

He blinked and turned back to the group surrounding him. Wesley was the one who'd tapped his shoulder. His brother's eyebrows were raised nearly to his hairline. "What's wrong?"

Tyrone shook his head. "Nothing, just got distracted for a second."

"Distracted," Dion said with a frown. "I thought you couldn't wait to do this investigation."

"I couldn't. I mean, I can't. My bad."

His brothers gave him one last confused look before they set up to redo the shot. Tyrone kept his mind on what they were there for and eventually was able to get his mind on the investigation, and off Kiera.

After a few minutes they set up inside with the home-owners, Ashlei and Curtis, to talk about what they'd experienced.

By the time they finished the discussion with the owners about the strange things in the home and walked through the house, Tyrone's heart rate mimicked a jackrabbit's—not just from the excitement of a new investigation, but from the weird vibe in the house. Something was happening there. Something that made his skin crawl and the muscles of his neck tighten. He wasn't as sensitive to the spirits they investigated as Wesley, but tonight he'd felt the animosity of whatever was in that house.

"What do you think is going on?" Dion asked when they'd finished the scene with the family and put their equipment in the back of the black SUV they drove for the show. He'd originally looked forward to spending the night in the house, but now that they'd spent time in there, he doubted he'd be able to even get ten good minutes of sleep.

"I don't know," said Wesley, who was sitting in the back hatch of the SUV. "Usually, it seems like the people haunting locations have a story to tell or want us to help them in some way. I didn't get that here."

Tyrone rubbed the back of his neck, which still tingled. It felt as if someone was watching—someone other than the camera crew filming their discussion. "It seems as if this spirit just wants to cause chaos."

"And terrorize this family," Dion said. He let out

a sigh before closing the box that held their equipment. "I'm not looking forward to spending the night here tonight."

Neither did Tyrone, but he wasn't about to admit to being afraid. Not with Kiera watching. He placed a hand on his brother's shoulder. "The three of us will be there. We'll be good."

They bumped fists and then got into the car so the camera could get a shot of them driving down the road. Later, when they were back at the hotel for a break before filming their overnight stay, Kiera came into the room they shared just as he was waking up from a nap.

She took one glance at him lying on the bed, staring at the ceiling, and put a hand to her chest. "My bad, did I wake you?"

He shook his head, pushed back the covers and sat up. "Nah, I just woke up." He rubbed his eyes. "Just thinking about the night ahead."

Kiera's eyes were on his bare chest. He'd taken off his shirt and wanted to strip to his underwear, but since they were sharing a room, he'd slipped on a pair of sweats. He wanted to feel cocky watching her stare at him, but knew she wouldn't follow up on her obvious interest because of his past.

After a few quick seconds, her eyes jumped to his. "Are you sure you're going to be okay? Usually, you and your brothers are excited about this part—today you all seem a little uneasy."

He shrugged before swinging his feet to the side of the bed. Because the hotel was busy, they'd been put in a room with two double beds. It was a blessing in disguise. If they'd had to share a king bed he would try to keep his distance, but knew just like when they'd shared the bed before he would still wake up with Kiera in his arms. With the distance currently between them having separate beds only made the loss of her pulling away even more potent.

"It's a weird vibe this time, that's all. But we'll be okay."

She sat on the other bed, facing him. "Are you sure?" She kept her eyes above his neck as she spoke.

"I'm sure. Don't worry, everything will be fine." He pushed aside the unease he'd felt earlier that day and tried to appear brave and positive. The last thing he wanted was for Kiera to worry about him. He only wanted her to see him as confident and capable.

She stared at him for several seconds before nodding and standing. He took her wrist in his before she could walk away. She looked down at him. "Thanks," he said.

A corner of her mouth lifted. "You're always saying thanks. What's it for this time?"

He stood, expecting her to step back, but she only shifted slightly to give him enough room to stand. Not far enough away for his hand to easily fall from her wrist. Not far enough away to prevent the tempting smell of her perfume to tickle his nose. "For caring and checking in on me. I know that's not part of the deal, but I do appreciate it."

"Why are you acting like it's unfamiliar to have someone care about you? It's obvious your brothers care about you, along with several people in your hometown."

"Yeah, they do, but with you it's different."

"Different how?"

"Just different." He didn't know how to explain that her concern sent a funny feeling through his chest. That knowing she cared made him want to do better, work harder, be safer. He didn't want her to worry, and that thought was slowly starting to impact nearly every decision he made.

She nodded and her smile softened. "I do care, so be careful, okay."

"I'm always careful."

She patted his bare chest. The warmth of her palm spread through his body. "And don't be afraid to speak up if things are too weird or you feel uncomfortable. There's nothing wrong with admitting that. You understand that, right?"

He'd been prepared to pretend as if he wasn't uneasy about spending the night in that house. To show her how he was fearless and ready to tackle whatever came his way. Instead, she'd seen right through him. Instead of viewing him as weak, she wanted to make sure he was okay.

He wasn't supposed to cross the line. She'd set a

boundary after their last talk, and he knew she'd done that to protect them both. Right now, that didn't matter.

Tyrone placed his hand on the back of her head and lowered his mouth to hers. He kissed her softly, pulling her lower lip between his. Once, twice and a third time. The kiss was long enough to satisfy the craving gnawing inside of him and brief enough to keep him from losing control, pulling her flush against him and falling to the one of the two beds with her in his arms.

He pulled back slowly. Kiera's eyes opened. Desire simmered in the depths of her gaze. He wanted to stoke the flames but held himself in check. Now wasn't the time to test the barriers she'd put up.

"Still, thank you. I promise. Everything will be good tonight."

Chapter Fifteen

Tyrone and his brothers sat around a table in the back of Stan's, a bar and grill two blocks from the beach. Stan's was a hole-in-the-wall frequented by locals and a few tourists who weren't interested in the fancier restaurants that catered to visitors. They'd met up at Stan's a few times over the years. Mostly when they wanted to get out and have a drink without dealing with a club or a huge crowd of people. Which was exactly what they needed tonight.

Tyrone took a long sip of his beer then let out a breath. "I didn't expect the investigation to go like that."

"I don't think any of us did," Wes said, slowly turning his bottle of beer on the table.

Dion straightened and looked at them both. "But

we did find an answer. They now know what they're dealing with and, hopefully, will get their kids out of that house."

They'd completed the investigation in Wilmington, and everyone had agreed to take a few days off afterward. Their research into the history of the place led them to believe the home was haunted by the ghost of a serial killer, who'd been killed in the house by one of the victims he'd kept there. Something the family hadn't known when they'd gotten the place at such a good price. The brothers had never come across something so angry, so malevolent, before. The anger and hatred permeating the atmosphere had kept the brothers up all night. The next morning they'd been so wired they could barely talk without snapping at each other. The entire crew had finished the investigation shaken.

"But will they, though?" Tyrone asked skeptically. "When you mentioned leaving the house the husband didn't seem too excited about the idea of moving."

Wesley snorted. "'We got the house at a good price,'" he said, mimicking Curtis's voice after they recommended moving or finding someone to expel the spirit.

Tyrone frowned into his beer. "Yeah, because it's haunted by a serial killer. One who liked to torture his victims. If they were smart, they'd move."

"Amen to that," Wes said. He held up his beer bottle and Tyrone clinked his own to Wes's.

"We can't control that," Dion said. "All we can do is give them the information they asked for. If they don't move, it's not on us." He met Wes's gaze, then Tyrone's. "Understand."

Wes sighed but nodded. "I understand."

Tyrone twisted his shoulders. The thought of the family staying in that house with that spirit put him on edge. He wanted to shake the husband for worrying more about having to move again, when it was obvious his wife and kids were petrified to spend another day in the house.

Dion bumped his hand. "Understand?"

Tyrone rubbed the bridge of his nose, then downed the rest of his beer. "I get it. I know it, but y'all have to admit the vibe in that house was off. They won't have any peace if they stay there."

"It had to be one of the worst places we've been in," Wes said.

Dion nodded. "I agree."

"But you're right, we helped them as much as we could," Tyrone said. "It's on them to figure out what to do next." All he could do now was hope and pray the family would move for the sake of their children.

Dion's cell phone rang. He pulled it from his back pocket and smiled at the screen. "Hold up. This is Vanessa." He got up from the table and answered the phone.

Tyrone pointed in the direction that Dion rushed off toward. "I thought we said brothers' night."

Wes chuckled and sipped his beer. "Vanessa is worried about him. She heard the way he sounded when he called after the investigation. Dion is telling us to chill, but this got to him just as much as us. I'm not surprised she called."

"How are you? I know you sense the emotions more than we do. You aight?"

Wes shrugged. "Yeah, I'll be fine." His cell phone rang before Tyrone could say anything else. He glanced at his screen and smiled sheepishly. "It's Cierra. I'll be right back."

Wes was up from the table and grinning into his phone in no time. Tyrone grunted and pulled out his phone. Nope, no missed calls. Not that he expected one. Kiera was his fake girlfriend. She wouldn't check on him to make sure everything was okay after a weird investigation. Not after he'd kissed her when she'd shown concern before their investigation. She'd offered comfort and he'd responded with a kiss. Nah, she wouldn't check in.

Still, he stared at his cell phone, willing it to ring. She was worried they'd end up like him and Sheri. A small part of him worried about that, too. He hadn't gone into this wanting a real relationship, but being with Kiera made him consider having a longer-term relationship. To be like his brothers and do the couple thing. Though he kind of wanted that, he also didn't want to mess up what he and Kiera had going by promising something he couldn't deliver. He knew himself. He loved being single, and he couldn't guarantee that one day he wouldn't meet someone else who interested him.

Basically, he was indecisive as hell.

Dion came back to the table first. "I'm going to head back home."

Tyrone frowned. "To Charlotte? I thought you were staying in Sunshine Beach tonight?"

"I was, but after talking to Vanessa I'm ready to get back. I don't want her to worry."

Tyrone sucked his teeth. "That goofy-ass grin on your face says something else. She ain't worried. You're ready to get home."

Dion laughed. "So, what if I am? I thought you'd be happy I wasn't in the way of you and Kiera."

Wes walked up before Tyrone could reply. "Hey, fellas, I'm gonna make it a night."

Tyrone's eyes widened and he threw up a hand. "You, too? We've only had one beer."

Wes shrugged. "Cierra knows how I get after an intense investigation. She's right. I need to decompress."

"Decompress?" Tyrone motioned to the table in front of him "Bruh, that's what we were doing?"

Wes shook his head and laughed. "Man, this means you can get back home to Kiera. Why are you making a big deal? I can tell you're just as anxious to see her."

"What?" Tyrone asked, his voice going up. He

wasn't anxious to see her. Anxious to talk to her maybe. Was it that obvious?

"The way you keep checking your phone is proof she'll be calling in a few, too." Wes threw some money on the table. "Let's get out of here and go home to our ladies."

"I'm down for that," Dion said with that silly grin.

Tyrone wanted to argue but kept his words to himself. Arguing about staying out would only alert his brothers. He still hadn't told them the relationship was fake and doubted he ever would. They were happy for him. As if they couldn't believe their playboy brother had finally settled down, but were happy he'd finally found someone. He didn't want to see the disappointment in their eyes that was sure to come if he told them he'd made up the whole thing. He'd come through with the show after years of being the indecisive, flighty, screwup of the three. They were finally starting to look at him like a respectable adult. Admitting his lie now would only have them go back to viewing him as a screwup.

The brothers hugged before getting in their vehicles and driving their separate ways. He'd looked forward to hanging with Wes and Dion. He missed them. He saw them more because of filming, but that was work. When they did get a rare break in filming, like today, they were ready to go back to their homes. He didn't blame them, since he liked Vanessa and Cierra, but he missed the days when it was just the three of them.

He laughed to himself. Two years ago, he would have scoffed if anyone said he would one day miss not having his brothers around constantly. After years of not wanting to be tied to Sunshine Beach and living in the shadows of his two older brothers, now he looked back with wistfulness. He had to laugh. He was really getting old.

Kiera's car was in the yard of the family home, but the front lights weren't on. He'd offered her the guest bedroom after filming so she wouldn't have to drive all the way back to Atlanta, and thankfully she'd agreed. He hoped she hadn't gone to bed yet. Now that his brothers bailed on him, he didn't want to be alone. He wasn't as sensitive to the entities they investigated, but he still hadn't completely shaken off the unease of before. He understood why his brothers has been so eager to get back to their homes, though. Now that he was here and knew Kiera was inside, he wanted what his brothers would have when they got home. To go inside, have Kiera ask if things were okay, sit and talk with her, go to sleep with her body against his. To feel reassured and secure in something good and comforting.

Sighing and feeling foolish for wanting something from Kiera he couldn't ask for, Tyrone went inside. The smell of freshly popped popcorn greeted him and his stomach growled. He followed the smell down the hall to where Kiera was sitting in the corner of the sectional in the family room. A large bowl of popcorn sat on the coffee table along with a two-liter bottle of cola, a bottle of rum and boxes of candy like they had at the movie theater. When he entered, she turned to look at him over her shoulder and smiled.

"Good, I timed it right," she said.

He cocked his head to the side. "Timed what?"

"When you'd get here," she said. "Vanessa and Cierra called me and let me know they'd broken up the boys' party. I knew you'd be coming home... Well, I hoped you'd be coming home. You had a rough time with the investigation." She pointed to the spread on the coffee table and then the television. "So, I planned for movie night."

He looked from the popcorn to the streaming service cued up on screen to her uncertain brown eyes. A vise tightened around his chest, making it hard to breathe, and he had to bite his lower lip to stop himself from having the same goofy-ass grin he'd accused Dion of having.

"You did all this for me?"

She waved a hand. "It's no big deal. I know you were looking forward to hanging out with your brothers. I can't replace them, but I hope I'm a good enough substitute."

He came around the couch and walked right up to her. He almost pulled her into his arms for a hug. The urge to do so was strong, he flexed his fingers. But he'd promised not to cross the line, and he'd already done that when he kissed her in their hotel room.

"You're the perfect substitute," he said instead of squeezing her tight against him, the way he wanted to.

Her smile was dazzling before she pointed to the spot on the couch next to her. "Then sit and let's watch."

Tyrone quickly sunk down into the cushions. "What are we looking at?"

"I figured a comedy was in order. I heard the superhero spoof that came out earlier this year was pretty good. That cool?"

He would watch a documentary on paint drying if she asked. He was just happy that she'd planned a date night for them. "That's cool."

For the first time since their talk about his past relationship, she didn't sit far away from him on the couch. Instead, she stayed right next to him. Not touching, but close enough for the heat of her body to comfort him and the sweet smell of her to relax the tension lingering in his body. She was dressed casually in a gray tank top and matching lounging pants. The pants were loose, but the flimsy material clung to her thighs. When she pulled her legs beneath her and leaned sideways to rest her head on the back of the couch, the front of her tank top dipped enough to give him an enticing view of her décolletage.

The vice tightened. His desire stirred to life, and he licked his lips. One way he'd previously eased tension after a weird investigation was by finding someone willing to spend the night with him. He shifted on the sofa and tried to gather his thoughts. He could do this. He was an adult. He did not need to have sex just to relax.

She turned to him, and he jerked his eyes away from her and back to the television. "Um… I heard this was funny, too," he said clearing his throat.

"Good. I hope it is."

The movie was hilarious. They laughed until their stomachs hurt as they shared popcorn and candy, and mixed up the rum with the cola. The best part was how she eased closer to him until their sides touched as they watched. When the movie ended an hour and a half later, he didn't want the night to end.

"One more? There's a historical that I wanted to check out?"

She frowned at him. "Historical? You like historical movies?"

He shrugged. "It's about the Negro leagues. I've always been interested. My dad said his great-grandfather used to play in them. Whenever a new movie comes out, I feel like I'm supporting my dad's legacy. He didn't get to tell me much about his great-grandfather before he died. Back then, I wasn't as interested in family history. I thought I had all the time in the world to know more."

He hadn't mentioned that to anyone in years. If ever. His parents were always trying to tell them about their family history. Instill in them a sense of pride of where they'd come from and what his ancestors had accomplished. Tyrone hadn't cared to listen to what he considered preaching. Now, he'd give anything to hear one more story.

Her eyes softened and she nodded. "Sure, let's watch that."

The second movie was good, but longer, and they'd both had two rum and colas. When she snored softly, and her head fell on his shoulder, he just smiled and adjusted his arm around her shoulder. Kiera snuggled in closer against his side. He planned to finish watching the movie, but when his head jerked up what felt like two minutes later, the credits were playing.

Kiera was still asleep in his arms, her body soft and warm against him. He hated to wake her. He'd rather sit there all night and hold her, but he didn't want her to wake up and feel uncomfortable.

He brushed a hand across her cheek. "Kiera," he said softly.

She wrinkled her nose and sighed before snuggling closer. The softness of her breasts, encased in a sports bra but still lush and tempting, pushed against his side. His penis stirred again. Shifting, Tyrone cleared his throat and shook her a little. "Kiera, wake up."

Her eyes drifted open. She blinked up at him, then smiled. "I'm awake."

He chuckled and ran his fingers over her cheek again because he just couldn't help himself. "You were out," he whispered.

She frowned and pursed her lips. "No, I wasn't. I was resting my eyes."

"Oh, that's what you call that snoring."

She grinned and lightly punched his chest. "I don't snore."

Tyrone wrapped his fingers around her wrist and rested her hand over his heart, which had started beating faster. "Okay, sure, we'll go with that."

She looked up at him, the smile still on her lips. Time seemed to stop, and Tyrone's breathing quickened as the smile on her face drifted away and something hot and tempting replaced the humor in her eyes. He shouldn't do it. He really should get up, walk up those stairs and go to bed alone. But when her fingers flexed against his chest and her tongue darted across her lower lip, instinct kicked down his defenses and he lowered his mouth to hers.

Chapter Sixteen

At first Kiera thought she was dreaming when she woke up in Tyrone's arms, but his mouth on hers was very real. The scratch of his goatee against her skin. The sweet heat of his tongue as it brushed across the seam of her lip. The softness of his breath as it mingled with hers. All of those things were better than anything she'd dreamed about.

For a second, she thought about pulling away. She had been vehement about keeping her distance from Tyrone. That she didn't want to be another broken heart in his wake. Then his hand slid up her side and cupped her breast, and she said to hell with her reservations and gave her body what it had craved since that first kiss that had ultimately landed them here.

Kiera relaxed into his strong embrace. His lips expertly traveled over hers, drawing her in and turning her body into mush with each sweet slide. He nipped and lightly sucked on her lower lip until she whimpered softly and pressed closer to him.

Tyrone shifted and pulled her into his lap. Kiera quickly rearranged her legs and straddled his hips. The warm heat of his skin as his hand slid up her shirt sent shivers through her body. His mouth trailed down the side of her neck to gently suck on the soft spot at the base of her throat. She gasped and clasped his shoulders when his tongue lapped across the same spot. His mouth stopped that sweet torture to trail light kisses across her chest to the tops of her breasts. Her nipples hardened and she pressed forward. She wanted his mouth on them.

His fingers skimmed her sides as he lifted her tank top. Cocooned in a sensual daze, she raised her arms so he could toss it over her head. Tyrone made quick work of the hooks of her sports bra. Her breasts spilled free, and Tyrone's eyes lit up as if he'd just discovered chocolate diamonds. His warm hands cupped her breasts, pushing them together and lifting them so his eager lips could close over the hard tips.

Pleasure exploded as his mouth made slow, sexy pulls on one nipple before sliding over to the other. Kiera's nails dug into his shoulders. She rotated her hips, pressing the heat of her sex against the hardness of his dick. The ensuing pleasure was delicious but not enough. Tyrone groaned and flicked his tongue lightly over one of her taut nipples. Kiera gasped and arched her back.

Tyrone looked up and met her eyes through lowered lids. "Tell me to stop now before I take you upstairs." His voice was low, sexy and made her sex clench.

She answered with a sly smile. "What are you going to do if you take me upstairs?" Definitely not the smart answer, but based on the spark in his eye that was the right answer.

He pulled her forward until her breasts were pressed against his chest, then whispered in her ear. "I'm going to slowly remove every inch of clothing you're wearing, kiss every part of your body until I stop to suck on your clit then slide all up in you and make love until we both pass out."

The rush of need that crashed through her body almost had her on her knees in front of him begging for every single thing he mentioned. She barely managed not to weep from the imagined pleasure. "You better live up to these words, sir."

The way his lips lifted in a cocky grin had her toes curling. "Oh, I'll deliver."

She squeezed her thighs against his. "Then prove it."

Tyrone stood with her still in is arms. He slowly lowered her so that her curves slid down every hard inch of his body. After another quick but thorough kiss, he took her hand and they sprinted up the stairs.

Once they were behind closed doors, he proceeded to quickly lay her on the bed. He studied her body as if she was a work of art, drawing his lower lip between his teeth after spotting her red, satin panties. He peeled those off to reveal the neat triangle of short hair covering her sex and sucked in a breath. The look in his eyes, a mixture of desire, admiration and reverence, made Kiera feel more beautiful, more wanted, than she'd ever felt with another lover. He didn't look like he simply wanted to possess her body—he looked like he wanted to savor and enjoy each moment. His lips trailed across her body, the soft whisper of his breath a tantalizing caress against her skin as he murmured compliments. He gently spread her legs so his lips and tongue could glide across her sex before he softly pulled the sensitive bud into the warm heat of his mouth. Her body bucked off the mattress. Her hands clenched his head as the sinfully slick caress of his actions took her body on a sensual ride.

Tyrone was turning out to be the lover she'd imagined and more. His moans nearly matched hers with each one of his carnal kisses. The pleasure grew, expanded and stretched, until she shattered in waves so intense, she almost forgot her name was Kiera Cox. Tyrone lay next to her, still fully dressed with a smug smirk on his face.

"Why are you looking at me like that?" she asked, poking him in the chest.

"Because you're beautiful after you come."

She grinned but her eyes narrowed. "Oh, you think you did something?"

"I'm pretty sure I did." He licked his lips.

Kiera's stomach clenched. She lifted up on her elbow and pushed him onto his back. "I've got a few tricks up my sleeve, too." She shimmied down his body and unbuttoned his pants.

"What you doing?" he asked in a thick voice while lifting his hips so she could pull down his pants.

"Wait and see." She grinned up at him then pulled down his underwear.

He sprang free, long and thick, and Kiera licked her lips. Her mouth closed over him, and his eyes rolled to the back of his head. Kiera's own desire flashed hot again as she brought him closer to the edge. Her mouth and tongue played up and down his erection until his fingers gripped the sheets and his feet pressed into the mattress. His breathing picked up and his hips bucked. Kiera pulled back before he climaxed.

Tyrone's eyes widened as he looked at her. "What…? You stopping…why?"

She just grinned as she straddled his hips. "Because I want this." She took his hard length in her hands. Grinning, he got a condom from the nightstand and quickly covered himself. Kiera slowly eased down on him.

Tyrone gripped her hips. "Damn, Kiera," he groaned between clenched teeth.

Kiera worked slowly up and down. Enjoying every single inch of him. She was on the edge again and wanted to crash over. Her hands trailed down the front of her body to where they were joined. She caressed and rubbed in tandom with her movements. Her head was thrown back and her eyes closed as she reveled in the delicious feel of his body joined with hers. Tyrone's big hands cupped her breasts. The blunt tips of his fingers caressed then pinched her nipples. The hint of pain on top of all that pleasure was her undoing. She shattered around him. His body flexed deep inside, and he cried out before she collapsed against his chest.

Kiera snuck out of bed early the next morning and went into the bathroom to take a shower. She softly hummed to herself as she lathered up and let the warm spray rain down over her body. A voice in the back of her head whispered she should have regrets about what happened the night before. That she should say last night was a night that shouldn't be repeated. The pleasurable memories of their lovemaking whispered and urged her to indulge for a little bit longer. So, that's what she'd do. They could talk out the ramifications of what they'd done like responsible adults later.

The door to the bathroom opened while Kiera was

in the middle of washing her face. Her eyes popped open, and she snatched back the shower curtain. Tyrone stood inside the bathroom, gloriously naked, with a teasing smile on his face.

"What are you doing in here?" she asked, wide-eyed. Her face was lathered, and she was wearing a blue shower cap. She was nowhere as glamorous or sexy as the smile on his face deserved.

"Joining you?" He came closer.

"But I'm washing my face," she said awkwardly.

"And I'll wash your back." He cocked his head to the side. "Do you want me to leave?"

"I look a mess. I don't have makeup on." She closed her eyes and cringed as soon as the words came out. She was supposed to be confident and secure around Tyrone. Not let her lingering adolescent insecurities show.

The soap on her face got into her eyes and she winced before darting back into the shower to rinse her face. Tyrone's chuckle preceded him as he got in behind her. The shower was small and barely fit the two of them, but when he pressed his hard body against her back and his long fingers massaged her sides while she rinsed the soap out of her eyes, she didn't care about the cramped space.

They lathered each other up. Each slippery caress, as his hands and fingers worked their way over her back, stomach and breasts, sent shivers of pleasure across her spine. She was more concerned with the way his stomach tensed at her touch, or the hard pounding of his heart against his chest, than she was with cleaning him off. By the time they'd rinsed off, her body trembled and ached for more.

They tried to make love in the shower but laughed as they struggled against the confines of the small space. Ultimately, they ended up back on the bed in a tangle of sheets, arms and legs. They made love fast and hard until Kiera lay panting and sated, ready to fall back asleep.

Tyrone leaned over and kissed her parted lips. "I'm going to make breakfast."

Kiera grinned and cracked open her eyes to see his face. "How can you move after that?"

His cocky grin made her want to flip him over and go for another round, but her stomach growled before she could indulge in the fantasy.

Tyrone placed his hand over her belly. "Because I've got to feed you if I'm going to work you out like that."

Kiera swatted at his head but he rolled away quickly. He laughed as she tossed a pillow his way. "You are so full of yourself."

He pulled a pair of sweatpants out of his drawer. "And you like it." He winked. "Waffles or pancakes?"

"Whatever you make I'm eating." She rolled over onto her stomach and hugged the other pillow.

He pulled his lower lip between his teeth and stared at her. "Damn, girl, you are sexy as hell."

Grinning, Kiera pointed toward the door. "Breakfast before round two."

He nodded and hurried over to kiss her quickly on the temple, then headed out the door. Kiera put a hand over her grin, but when her fingers ran across her bare face, her eyes popped open. She pressed both hands to her cheeks then groaned. She had to look awful. No makeup and somehow her blue shower cap had remained on her head. There was nothing she could do about that now. He'd seen her without makeup and still found her sexy. She might as well get over it.

Kiera took her time styling her short hair into a sleek bob and putting on makeup, then dressed in the lounge pants she'd worn the night before and a comfortable T-shirt. The smells of coffee and cinnamon greeted her downstairs.

"Okay, there's no pancake or waffle mix. And while I believe we have everything to make it from scratch, that's more Wes's lane. So I improvised." He slid a plate with a slice of the cinnamon bread she liked onto her place at the table. "Cinnamon bread for you and cereal for me." He grabbed the bowl of cereal off the counter.

"Cinnamon toast is fine. Thank you." She poured a cup of coffee before sitting with him.

"We don't have to shoot today," he said.

She nodded and took a bite of the bread. "I know. I'm glad. You and your brothers need a few days to recoup after that last investigation."

"Then why did you put on makeup?"

She glanced away and shrugged. "I like makeup. Nothing wrong with that."

"I know, but you also said you weren't wearing makeup when I came into the bathroom as if you were worried."

She reached for the stick of butter and the butter knife he had to have put on the table for her earlier, and spread some on her toast. "You caught me off guard. That's all."

"You know I've seen you without makeup on, right."

Her eyes shot to his. "What? When?" She'd tried to discreetly always be ready before he got up in the mornings and she kept a mask on her face on the nights they shared a room.

"Kiera, we've shared a room multiple times. I've seen you in the middle of the night when that mask you wear comes off. And, believe it or not, I've caught glimpses of you in the mornings or evenings before you've put on makeup and taken it off."

Her shoulders stiffened. "Is this when you tell me that I don't need makeup, it makes me look fake and I shouldn't wear it?"

He held up a hand. "Nah, you do what you want. It's your face. I'm just curious about why you don't want me to see you without it. I mean…you are beautiful regardless."

She glared at him. "You can spare me the heart-warming words. I know you're just being nice."

He glared back as if her words insulted him. "I'm for real. I'm not going to tell you to go out without makeup or anything. I think you're sexy as hell when you're all done up. I just want you to feel comfortable with me."

"Why?"

"Because I'm comfortable with you."

His simple words took the fight out of her. She'd had plenty of people tell her she "didn't need makeup" or that she should "be more natural." She always wanted to tell those people to mind their own damn business. Sometimes she did. She was glad Tyrone's default was "live life on your own terms." Maybe that's why he simply wanted to understand versus telling her to do things differently.

She sipped her coffee and nibbled on her toast before responding. "I told you about the acne when I was a kid, right?"

"Yeah, I remember."

"I didn't tell you about the teasing that went with it. Or the scars the acne left. I've done what I could to minimize them and make them less noticeable, but I still feel…uncomfortable with going out without something covering them."

"I'd never tease you about that," he said, again sounding affronted by the idea.

Kiera smiled and nodded. "I know. I also know most people wouldn't say a word or even judge me by them, but I just prefer to put my best face forward. I'm going to be judged on so much already. Being a woman, being Black, being in debt, being a makeup artist. I don't want to add one more thing for people to judge me by."

He reached out and placed his hand over hers. He interlaced their fingers and gave a light squeeze. "Just know when you're here and when you're with me, you don't need to worry about being judged. I like *you*. Not just the way you look."

His words wiggled through her keep-my-emotions-out-of-this armor and sunk into her heart. Could she really spend her nights making love to him and not get sucked into wanting him forever? She pushed away that thought. Focused on the present. She'd enjoy the moment with no expectations and no dreams of happily-ever-after. That's how she'd get through this unscathed.

She pulled back her hand and cupped her coffee mug. "I appreciate that." She took a sip. "I also like you for who you are."

He grinned. "I appreciate that, too."

"Oh, really? I mean, as the adored baby boy of the family you must be used to people liking you," she teased to get them back in playful territory. Their relationship wasn't about making deep and personal confessions.

"Adored, maybe. But also judged as being temperamental and unreliable. I'm working to change that. I think my brothers are finally starting to see me as a fully functioning adult and not the hotheaded teenager I used to be."

"Like I said before, you're passionate. Maybe sometimes too much, but you also listen to reason when people approach you. Your brothers know that about you and from where I sit, they care about you and want to look out for you. I don't see them judging you or viewing you as unreliable. You always seem to come through when it counts."

He sat up straighter. "You really think that?"

She nodded slowly. "I do."

"You're good for me, Kiera. I like that about you." He looked down at his cereal. "Ugh, this is soggy. Let me get some more." He got up and went to the sink.

Kiera stared down into her coffee. He'd meant the words as a compliment, but they didn't hit that way. She didn't want to just be good for someone—she wanted to be wanted and loved by someone. She'd remember that as she played this foolish game of sex and fake romance with him. She may be good for Tyrone, but that didn't mean he was good for her.

Chapter Seventeen

The knock on Kiera's apartment door caused the lively conversation between Tyrone, his brothers, Vanessa and Cierra to stop as everyone turned toward the door. Tyrone clapped his hands. "Is that the food?"

Kiera held out her phone and waved it from side to side. "Yep, the app says my driver has arrived with the food." She jumped up from where she'd been sitting on one of the three beanbags she used as extra chairs. "I've got it."

"I'll help you." Tyrone got up from his beanbag beside her and followed her to the door.

Wesley laughed. He was stretched out on the love seat with one arm across the back and Cierra curled against his side. "You just can't stand to not have Kiera beside you for a moment. Love to see it."

Tyrone waved off his brother. "Mind your business."

Vanessa pointed at Wesley. She and Dion were similarly snuggled together on the sofa. "You see he didn't deny it, though."

The group laughed. Prickles of heat danced across Kiera's cheeks and neck. Tyrone was playing the loving, devoted boyfriend in front of his family. They'd continued their fake-couple-with-benefits relationship, but Kiera had intentionally avoided asking if the sleeping together meant anything. They were enjoying each other, but planned social-media posts, being affectionate when others were around and scheduling public appearances were still the main parts of their relationship.

Tyrone only chuckled at Vanessa's observation and his family burst out into knowing laughter. Kiera continued to the door and took the food from the delivery driver. They'd wrapped up one of the last investigations of the season in Atlanta. Tiana thought it was a good idea to include Vanessa and Cierra in the Atlanta filming. She'd set things up to have the two ladies arrive "unexpectedly" to surprise the brothers with a trip to Six Flags after their investigation.

The investigation of a home built in a neighborhood on the site of a former orphanage hadn't been easy. Thankfully, the spirits of the children were precocious and wanted to play, rather than torment the people living there. There'd been no evidence of foul play in any of the deaths but learning of an outbreak of diphtheria had still left the brothers more subdued afterward.

The Six Flags trip had proven to be a smart move. They'd gotten great footage of the three brothers enjoying life with their significant others. For a moment, Kiera had almost believed she was a real part of the family, which is why she'd invited everyone to hang out at her place afterward when they mentioned not wanting to deal with a crowd at a restaurant.

"This smells good," Tyrone said with a grin as they put the bags of food on the counter in Kiera's small kitchen.

"It does, and I'm hungry enough to eat it all," Kiera agreed. She breathed in the savory scent of steamed crab legs and shrimp from the various bags.

Vanessa came into the kitchen. "I think we all could eat everything on that counter. What can we help you with?"

Cierra also entered, then went to the sink and squirted hand soap into her palm. "Where are your plates? Do you have any old sheets or towels we can put down, so we don't mess up your furniture?" she asked as she washed her hands.

Kiera nodded. "I do. If you all will separate who ordered what I'll get some things to put down. Sorry I don't have a dining-room table we can sit around."

Cierra shrugged as she dried her hands on a paper

towel. "Girl, we don't care about that. We're just glad you let us hang out here."

"Exactly," Vanessa agreed. She went to the sink after Cierra moved out of the way.

"I'll get the stuff for the living room," she said.

Tyrone glanced at her. "You need help."

"Nah, you help them. I'll get your brothers to help spread out the towels. We'll turn the coffee table into a makeshift dining table."

Kiera went to the closet where the towels and sheets were kept and grabbed an old set of sheets. She brought them out and Dion and Wesley were quick to help her spread everything out.

"Oh, yeah, this is a good idea," Wesley said grinning. "Tyrone can't eat crab legs without flinging juice everywhere."

"I heard that. And you're the one who flings," Tyrone called from the kitchen.

They all laughed and quickly had the coffee table and the floor around it covered. Pretty soon the various bags of steamed crab legs, shrimp, sausage and corn were passed out. Everyone was ready to eat, but Tyrone still lingered in the kitchen.

Kiera pointed to the food. "Y'all start, I'll see what he's doing." She stood.

Dion shook his head. "We'll wait. We'll bless the food together."

"Be right back." She hurried toward the kitchen. "Hey, what's the holdup? Everyone is ready to eat."

She froze just inside the kitchen. Tyrone was staring down into her open junk drawer. His eyebrows drew together and he frowned. Kiera hurried over and pushed the drawer shut.

"What are you doing?"

"Your medical bills are that high?" She understood the disbelief in his voice. She'd felt the same way when they'd first started rolling in.

She glanced over her shoulder to make sure no one had followed then glared at him. "Can we talk about this another time? Your family is here, and they don't want to talk about my foot surgery."

His lips pinched together but he nodded. "I was looking for forks."

She opened the drawer next to the one for junk and bills she didn't want to deal with. "Here."

She didn't have a reason to be, but she was embarrassed that he'd seen that. She'd already told him she was working her way out of debt. Her needing money wasn't a surprise, it was the reason why she'd agreed to be his girlfriend for the show in the first place. She just hadn't expected him to look so…astounded to see the amount for himself. She was fairly lucky. The hospital had agreed to reduce her bill after she'd negotiated her payment, but that small negotiation didn't do much to combat the cost of foot surgery when she'd lacked health insurance.

He took out enough forks for everyone. "Thanks." He hesitated instead of leaving the kitchen. "I really wasn't trying to snoop. I saw the bill and spoke without thinking. I didn't mean to embarrass you."

"I forgot it was in there," she said. "It is what it is. You know as well as I that I'm doing what I can to pay it off."

He cringed as if her words were unpleasant. Kiera stared back into his eyes, unflinching. As much as they were enjoying the with-benefits portion of their relationship, the truth was the truth. After a second he relaxed and smiled. "Let's get back out there."

She nodded and followed him into the living area. Everyone grinned at them when they entered. Kiera and Tyrone settled onto the floor around the coffee table.

Kiera eyed the sly, knowing smiles on everyone's faces. She checked her clothes and patted her face to see if there was something on her she'd missed. "What?"

Wes shook his head and smirked. "Nothing."

Tyrone narrowed his eyes. "Nah, it's not nothing. What were y'all talking about?"

"Nothing, man," Dion said with a grin that undermined his words. "We were just talking about how happy we are for you two."

Tyrone reached for his food and pulled it closer to him. "Huh?"

Wes shrugged. "We were telling Dion how wrong he'd been."

Kiera untied the knot on the bag of her steamed seafood. "About what?"

"About you two not being in a real relationship," Vanessa said. "He thought you made it up for the show. But it was pretty obvious from the start that you two really care about each other. We're happy to see it."

"Yeah," Wes said, shaking his head as he slipped on the plastic gloves that came with their order. "I didn't think I'd see Tyrone settle down anytime soon. It's like Dad used to say, when you find the right person, you know." He leaned over toward Cierra with pursed lips. She grinned and kissed him quickly.

Dion grinned at Vanessa. "Amen to that."

Kiera and Tyrone shared a look. He gave her a soft smile. The affection in his eyes seemed so real that her heart squeezed, but he was only smiling like that so they wouldn't tip off his family. She looked away quickly and breathed in the enticing aroma from her bag. "Let's eat before it gets cold."

Kiera's cell phone rang while she and Tyrone washed the few dishes they'd used while his family was over. They'd eaten, laughed some more, debated politics and discussed the plotline of the thriller show on a streaming channel Wes had insisted they all watch, before Wes, Dion and their partners left thirty minutes prior. All in all, it had been a fun night.

She pulled her cell from her back pocket and cringed. Tyrone raised an eyebrow. "Who is it?"

"My mom?" She continued to frown at her phone.

She looked as if she'd been caught with her hand in the cookie jar. "Okay, I thought you got along with her."

"I do." She bit the corner of her lip and tossed the dishrag into the soapy water. "I'll be right back."

Tyrone watched as she hurried out of the kitchen. She never talked to her family in front of him. He understood at first. They weren't really a couple, and she didn't want her family to get involved. But after spending the evening with his family, talking and laughing, he found himself wanting to get to know her family. To meet the brother who made her eyes crinkle with humor whenever they texted. The dad who made her laugh out loud as she told stories of him and his friends and their rituals on football Sundays. The mom who made Kiera's voice fill with pride whenever she talked about her.

Her family obviously was a huge influence in her life, and she loved them. He wanted to know the people who loved her. Even more, he wanted to know if they would like him. Would they notice how much he wanted to make her happy?

He blinked and shook his head. "What in the world?" he muttered. Was he really starting to think this was real?

He had a second of disbelief followed immediately by the whisper of "why not" in his ear. Tyrone froze in the middle of drying the glasses Kiera had washed before stepping out. He eased back from the sink and absently wiped his hands on a towel while those two words bounced around his head.

Why not? They liked each other. They were sleeping together. They made a good team together on the show. She didn't give him any grief about his past or the women he'd dated. So, for real, why not? He'd never gotten into a serious relationship because he'd never hooked up with someone he could imagine spending all of his time with. He didn't want his time with Kiera to end.

He nodded as the possibilities of "why not?" settled in and got comfortable in his head. A smile spread on his lips despite his heart rate picking up. He couldn't imagine Kiera being against it. She'd been interested in him from the start. She might hesitate a little, but he was sure she'd eventually see this made sense. Just as she'd done when he proposed they pretend to be dating, she'd realize that them being together had just as many benefits.

Emboldened by the idea, he dropped the towel and headed toward the living area. He wanted to tell her immediately. He felt like the smitten guy Dion and Wes accused him of being earlier in the night and he liked it.

"Ma, you don't need to meet him. I don't even know if this is going to last long, alright."

Kiera's voice stopped him in is tracks. Her back was to him as she stared out of the window. One hand pressed the phone to her ear the other was rubbing her temple.

"I don't mean anything is wrong now," she said. "I just mean we're dating but that doesn't mean you need to start planning weddings or anything. Can we just treat him like any other guy I've dated?"

Tyrone scowled. Weddings? He wasn't ready to discuss weddings. But the like-any-other-guy comment really had him confused. He most definitely was not like any other guy.

"You know what I mean. You never met Mike and was okay with that. You just want to meet Tyrone because you like his show."

Mike? Who the hell was Mike?

"Fine, I'll get their autographs, but can you please let me figure this out. I don't want you and Dad to get all excited about this. Tyrone is cool, but we're not headed toward anything serious. Rodrick and Contessa will get married before we ever will." There was a pause as her mom talked and then Kiera let out a dry laugh. She dropped her hand from her temple to her hip. "Pretty much. He's my for-now guy, okay. You understand that, don't you?" Another pause before Kiera nodded. "Thank you. Now, I've got to go. I had friends over and I need to clean up. Nah, just some of the ladies I haven't seen in a while. We're traveling tomorrow to finish shooting, so I won't get to drop by. I'll call you later. Okay. Love you, too. 'Bye."

Kiera ended the call and sighed. She slid her phone in the back pocket of her pants and turned. Their eyes met and she froze.

"Oh, hey, you done with the dishes?"

"Yeah…" he scratched his chin then walked over to her. "What does your 'for-now guy' mean?"

Her eyes widened. "Huh… Oh, that." She waved a hand and chuckled. "You know. The person I'm with for now."

"That's what I am?"

She nodded slowly and looked at him as if he should already know the answer to that question. He did, but he didn't like hearing it out loud. "Yeah. That's the whole reason we're doing this."

He watched her and waited. Waited for a sign that she was starting to think along the same lines as he was. That maybe she was also on this why-not train sending him off the rails.

"I mean," he said slowly. "That's how it started…. but…"

She stepped forward and wrapped her arms around his neck. Tyrone's hands automatically rested on her hips. His thoughts scattered with her soft curves pressed against him.

Kiera stared up at him with beautiful, serious brown eyes. "I know we crossed the line when we slept together, but don't worry. I'm keeping my head on straight and I know what this is."

"But what if—"

She lifted on her toes and kissed him, further scattering the words he'd been about to utter. She knew what it did to him when she lightly sucked on his bottom lip like that.

"Don't worry," Kiera whispered against his lips. She spoke softly as she placed light kisses across his jaw. "I won't mix things up. My heart is safe, and I won't be keying your car," she said with a light chuckle. "The season is almost over. Let's keep having fun while we get through this."

The keying-his-car comment pushed back the desire rising in him. Would he ever outlive that? "I'm not worried about you keying my car. I'm—"

"Good." She brushed her lips over his. This time her tongue traced across his lower lip. "Now let's make a good night even better."

One of her hands slid from his shoulder, down his chest, across his abdomen and stopped at the waistband of his pants. Her fingers made quick work of the button there.

He grinned as desire surged forward, knocking his doubts out of the way and honing in on the naughty look in her eye. "What are you doing?"

Her soft lips brushed over his jaw down to his neck. "You know what I'm doing." Her teeth nipped at the pulse pounding in his throat.

Tyrone's body trembled and thoughts of a longer, deeper conversation faded as her hand slipped into his underwear and her warm fingers clasped around him. He brought a hand to the back of her head and deepened the kiss. When she slightly squeezed his length, he gasped and became putty in her hands.

He felt her smile against his lips. "You okay with that?"

"Hell yes," he said.

"Good."

Kiera's body brushed his as she lowered to her knees in front of him. Tyrone let his worries about meeting her family and thoughts of serious talks fade. No way was he letting her go. He'd figure out a way to make her feel the same.

Chapter Eighteen

Kiera couldn't believe filming for the second season was over so soon, yet there they were going to the wrap party. The past ten weeks had passed by in a blink. Despite the whirlwind of a schedule, traveling to different locations for the investigations and the upheaval of her life because of her agreement with Tyrone, Kiera was a little sad to see the end. She'd enjoyed working with the rest of the cast and crew to make the show happen. Even though her part was to make Tyrone look better, she was still proud of the work they'd done and was excited to see the final product on screen.

She and Tyrone arrived at the party, which was being held at a seafood restaurant on the harbor in Sunshine Beach, just after 7:00 p.m. Not quite fashionably late and not too early to be considered overly eager. The party was small with just the brothers, their friends and the crew members. Because it was casual Kiera had opted for an off-the-shoulder white sweater, fitted dark jeans and heels. Her hair was flat-twisted into a simple yet complementary updo. Tyrone also went simple with a black crewneck sweater and gray pants that accentuated his thighs in a not-so-simple manner. His hair and goatee were neatly trimmed, and he'd put on the cologne that made her want to curl up into his arms and breathe in his scent.

The rest of the crew greeted them when they entered. They stopped to speak, take selfies and congratulate everyone on a great ending to another season before finding Dion, Vanessa, Wes and Cierra at the bar with beers in their hands.

Tyrone slapped hands with Wesley and then Dion. "Another successful season."

Kiera grinned and ran her hand up and down his back. She'd gotten comfortable with easily touching him whenever they were around people. "With more to come."

Vanessa pointed at Kiera. "Amen to that."

Dion rubbed a hand over his stomach and gave them an anxious look. "I hope so."

Tyrone caught the bartender's attention, pointed at Dion's beer and then at himself. "We don't have to hope about more seasons." He looked at Kiera. "What would you like?"

"Same is good."

He held up another finger to indicate two beers. When the bartender nodded, he turned back to them. "I got a feeling this will definitely turn into a season three," Tyrone said to Dion. "There's already buzz from the fans about this upcoming season, and we haven't even begun to air promos. We've gained popularity. That has to be a good thing."

Wes waved a finger. "Hold up. We haven't gotten anything. The popular ones are you and Kiera. The fans love y'all and your social-media posts and fan interactions during the replays of last season's shows. We owe a lot of this success to you two."

Kiera shook her head. "We just helped start a conversation. The real success is the three of you. Never forget that."

Cierra rubbed Kiera's arm. "True, but you won't hold it against me if I pray for you and Tyrone to stay together for a long time."

The smile on Kiera's face froze in place. She'd kept Tyrone away from her family because she hadn't wanted them to become attached. Until this moment, she hadn't thought about Tyrone's family becoming attached to her. With his dating history, she'd assumed they would move on and forget about her after they parted ways. The hopeful look on Cierra's face, and the rest of his family's eyes, told another story.

She let out a shaky laugh that she hoped didn't sound as stiff to them as it felt for her. "I won't hold it against you" was all she could think of as a response.

Tyrone placed a hand on the small of her back. "Neither will I."

He met Kiera's eyes and her heart stuttered. He had that look again. She'd seen that look a few times since they'd started sleeping together. The look that said he was starting to think this arrangement they had was a good idea for the foreseeable future. The look that meant he'd taken his you're-good-for-me feeling and convinced himself he needed to keep her by his side. It was a look she didn't trust at all.

They were interrupted by Tiana. "My favorite brothers! Congratulations on another fantastic season. I knew you would be a hit."

"I appreciate that, Tiana," Tyrone said. "You believed in us from the start."

She raised her glass of wine to him. "It was hard not to believe in you. You were passionate right from the start. I know a good thing when I see it." She looked at Kiera and winked. "This season is going to be even better than the last."

Other members of the crew followed her over and pretty soon talk about how great Kiera and Tyrone were together were lost in the fun and laughter of the evening. Kiera stuffed herself with the variety of oysters, one of the restaurant's signature delicacies, peel-and-eat shrimp, salmon and cake. Conversation flowed easily in between the toasts given to congratulate everyone who'd had anything to do with the show.

After the official thank-you speeches were given, the party settled down and everyone broke up into small groups. Kiera was sitting with Vanessa and Cierra discussing makeup with Tiana when Tiana's cell phone vibrated. She glanced at the screen and then her eyes widened.

"Oh, my god!" Tiana exclaimed.

The three other women stopped talking. Kiera's eyebrows raised. Her interest was piqued by the obvious excitement on Tiana's face. "What happened?"

Tiana shook her head. "Nothing to me. Not really. I forgot about a friend who's starting a reality show in LA. Shooting starts in a few weeks, but her makeup artist quit. She asked me if I knew someone. I told her about you, but with everything happening, I forgot to mention it. Are you interested?"

Kiera blinked, stunned. "Aren't makeup artists in LA a dime a dozen?"

Tiana shrugged off her words. "Exactly why she asked me for someone who's good and reliable. She's worked with the previous artist for years, but she got sick and can't do this and she didn't want to have to search for someone else. Haven't you tried to break out into bigger shows? Well, this one is a great one to work on."

"Are they paying?" Kiera asked.

"Of course, and more than what we paid," Tiana said with a raised eyebrow.

Vanessa and Cierra both grinned and slapped hands. "More money? That's what I'm talking about," Cierra said cockily.

Kiera stared at the two women whom she'd come to admire over the course of working on this show. They'd been nothing but friendly and supportive since she'd met them. Not having sisters, she could easily imagine they'd become like sisters to her if she'd really been dating Tyrone. Thinking she wouldn't miss them had been a gross miscalculation on her part.

She looked back at Tiana's expectant expression. She didn't have to think hard about her answer. "I'm interested."

Tiana clapped her hands. "Great! I'll text her now." Her fingers flew across the phone. A few seconds later, it buzzed again. "She'll call you later, but can you be in LA in two weeks?"

"For more money, I can be in LA tomorrow," Kiera said with a grin.

Everyone laughed as Tiana responded to the text. "I'm going to send her your number. I'm so glad this worked out. You know I'm always about helping other women be awesome."

Kiera clasped her hands together. She wasn't sure how much more they were paying, but working this job had allowed her to put a dent in her hospital bills and have more cushion when it came to her other expenses. Anything more would only make her goal of climbing out of debt that much easier.

Tyrone tapped her on the shoulder. She grinned up at him. "What's up?"

"Can we talk for a second?" He nodded at the rest of the group. "You ladies don't mind?"

"Only if you bring her back. We've got to celebrate," Vanessa said.

Tyrone's smile stiffened along the edges. "Yeah, I heard."

Kiera kept her face pleasant even though unease tickled her stomach. He couldn't possibly be upset about her being interested in the LA job. He couldn't be. He'd seen the bills and knew why she'd agreed to this outlandish scheme in the first place. He had to understand her interest.

He led her outside to the restaurant's deck, which overlooked the harbor. Sailboats and pleasure boats bobbed lazily in the water on the other side of the boardwalk. The sun had set, and moonlight glinted off the surface of the water. The smell of salt water drifted on the cool breeze. Tyrone pulled her over to one corner, where they couldn't be overheard.

"What's wrong?" she asked.

"Nothing…it's just." He shuffled from foot to foot before stopping to meet her gaze. "Are you going to LA?"

She glanced away to hide her disappointment. So,

this was about the LA job. "I don't know. If they offer me the job, then yeah."

"What about us?"

"The season is over."

"Filming is over, the season hasn't aired. We'll still need to make a few appearances to promote the show."

She nodded. "I understand that. Everyone will understand why I'm not around because of my job. Plus..."

His eyebrows drew together. "Plus what?"

"Plus, it'll be a good way for us to find a way to end this without issues." The way they'd originally planned. A mutual breakup that was handled professionally and courteously, so that neither would receive backlash.

Tyrone took a half step back. "You're thinking of ending this?" His voice was tight and full of disbelief.

"Tyrone, we both knew this wasn't forever." She leaned closer and lowered her voice. "Did you forget why we started?"

He stepped forward, closing the distance between them and putting a hand on her hip. He pulled her body closer. "That kiss is why we started."

His body was hard and warm, and she immediately responded. She trembled and her knees seemed to wobble. The man knew how to make her react. "Yeah, a kiss that almost ruined your second season and prompted you to ask me to be your fake girl-friend."

His other hand lifted and trailed over her cheek. "A kiss that proved from the start that we were good together. I was thinking we should keep this going?"

And there it was. The words she'd seen in his eyes before, but had found a way to keep him from uttering. "Why?"

"Why not?" he responded with a confident grin.

She pushed out of his embrace, frustrated that he would think this was that easy. That he would believe all it took was an embrace and half a smile, and she'd forget the dozens of red flags flying over a relationship with him. "Not 'why not.' Why should we keep this going?"

"Because I'm feeling you. I'm feeling us. We're good together." He spoke as if that was all it took to make a relationship work.

"You're feeling me and we're good together," she said in a calm voice. Not because he cared for her. Not because he wanted to really be her man. Not because he loved her, but because of what she'd feared. He loved the idea of her.

Maybe that was all he thought it took. He'd spent his life casually dating and not having to give much else. How could he understand that she needed more? Right now they were good together because they were pretending to be in love. They weren't really dealing with the things that could trip up a relationship. They were constantly the best, most under-standing versions of themselves. If they kept this going, then the real faults would show, and she didn't think they would make it.

"The only thing this has proven is that we're good at pretending to be together and having sex. What happens when you don't need me for the show, or you meet another woman you're interested in sleeping with?"

He scoffed and waved a hand. "Who says I'm going to sleep with someone else?"

"Are you saying you're ready to not sleep with anyone else for the rest of your life?"

That wiped the confident look off his face. He stepped back. "The rest of my life? I wasn't talking about the rest of my life."

"Then what are you talking about? Another few weeks, a few months, a year. What exactly are you asking me for?"

He stared back, stunned for a second, then began speaking. But this time his voice wasn't as sure. "For us to… I don't know. Not be fake anymore."

"You think you want that because right now is fun and we're doing well. But it takes more than that to make a relationship work."

He reached for her. "Come on, Kiera. We *are* good together. There's no need to stop."

She pulled out of his reach. "Yes, there is. I have to protect myself. Not just now but in the future. I did this to make money and I'm going to LA to make money. I'm not about to get caught up in your fantasy for longer than necessary."

"Kiera—"

She held up a hand. "Please, don't do this. Let's get through the start of the season as we planned, okay. Let's not further complicate things. I like you, Tyrone, and I want to keep liking you when this is over. If we drag this out longer than necessary then I might not be able to do that when we part ways."

He stared back. Even in the darkness she could see the confusion on his face. But along with the confusion there was also uncertainty. Her words had struck home and given him pause. He liked this idea for now, but that didn't mean he'd really thought about what them dating would look like. Maybe if he'd said he was willing to try, that he wasn't worried about tomorrow because all he wanted and needed today was her, she might have considered his options. But he hadn't. He'd tossed the idea out there as if it was a whim he'd pondered but hadn't taken seriously until she'd threatened to leave town. Frankly, she deserved more than that.

"Let's go back into the party," she said. "I need thank Tiana for helping me out."

She waited for him to argue more. For him to make another play for her. He didn't—he just nodded, placed his hand on the small of her back and they went back inside.

Chapter Nineteen

Tyrone maneuvered through the crowd in the club toward the VIP tables in the back. He raised his hands—one of which held drinks, a glass of wine for Kiera and a rum and Coke for him—to greet those who called out his name or spoke. He'd already done the rounds and had the talks with his old friends and colleagues from the radio station, so he didn't feel the need to stop and chat. His focus was getting back to Kiera sitting at their VIP table.

This was their date night. A date night to get promo pictures of them together before the season aired, but he hoped to use it for another reason. His goal was to take this time to try and convince Kiera to date him despite her concerns that he wasn't for real.

He'd thought the backstage passes and after party

was the perfect idea, until they'd arrived backstage and his former coworker, Towanda, had hugged him. He and Towanda had enjoyed a friends-with-benefits relationship. He'd worried things would get weird like with Sheri, but Towanda hadn't said a word and Kiera hadn't shown any hints of jealously. She never did, and that was another reason why she was perfect for him.

He made his way to their table. Kiera smiled at him as he approached. Every time he looked at her, she took his breath away. Tonight, she wore a black bustier top that had all of her sexy shoulders and décolletage out with a pair of tight, faux leather pants that clung to her hips and ass and made his hands flex with the memory of clutching them when they made love. He couldn't keep his eyes off her and had a hard time keeping his hands to himself.

She held out a hand for her wine. "Thank you."

"You're very welcome." He slid onto the leather couch next to her. "The show is about to start."

Her eyes lit up. "A show? But she just did a concert."

"You can't have an after party without at least one song," he said.

Her delighted wiggle as she took a sip of her wine made him want to request an entire set. She'd once mentioned she was a fan of the R&B singer, Jessica Stone. When he found out she was having a concert in Myrtle Beach, he'd immediately called in a favor to his friends at the radio station for tickets and VIP seats at the after party. He'd surprised Kiera with the date.

Her happy shimmy brought her body closer to him. He placed his hand along the back of the couch and ran his thumb across the smooth skin on the back of her shoulder. "You didn't get enough at the concert?"

"I did, but that doesn't mean a thing. Hearing her sing here is up close and personal." She leaned over and placed her head on his shoulder. "Thank you so much for this."

He wanted to take the arm on the back of the couch and pull her against him, but she sat up just as quickly as she'd leaned against him. She stared expectantly at the stage in the middle of the club.

"No problem at all," he said, trying to hide his disappointment. "I remember you mentioned how much you like her songs. You've got them playing almost all the time in the house."

She chuckled and took a sip of her drink. "Yeah, I do play her songs a lot. I've loved her ever since I was a teenager. Her songs about wanting love, her realness about being insecure about her looks and her struggle with self-love. I felt that as I was growing up."

"Her songs have changed in the last few years. They're a lot happier."

"I've seen some of her recent interviews. She is a lot happier. She's always been open about her struggles and she was open about the things she's done to heal. It's even helped me learn to be okay with myself."

He studied her face and couldn't imagine her not seeing just how beautiful she was. Tonight, her makeup was flawless and made her absolutely stunning. Without makeup she was still alluring. The scars left from her teens has faded and were only a small part of her.

"Do you still struggle with that?"

She took another sip and lifted a shoulder. "Not as much. I mean, you know I'm still not completely comfortable with going out without makeup, but I don't think I'm ugly anymore."

"You're not ugly," he said immediately. The thought of her thinking she was made him want to shower her with compliments.

She smiled and lifted a hand. "I know that. I did say 'anymore.' When I was a teen I thought I was, then I thought I was when it wasn't wearing makeup, and now I know that I am attractive. Makeup makes me feel even more attractive and I like that feeling."

He took her hand in his and lifted it to his lips. "You're also confident, sexy and extremely talented."

Her light laughter sent shivers across his skin. "Thank you. I will not deny any of those compliments. Especially the talented one."

"I've always wanted to have a talent," he said.

"You do have a talent. You're on television."

"I mean, like a tangible talent. Dion was always good with his hands and at sports. Wes is smart, can draw and design anything. My talent was getting on people's nerves."

Kiera covered her mouth with her laugh. "Stop it! You're cute and charming."

He wiggled his eyebrows. "Cute *and* charming?"

She rolled her eyes. "I was going to say humble at times, but…"

Tyrone chuckled, then nodded. "Alright, alright. I'll stop fishing. But you know what I mean. I can talk my way out of or into a lot of things, but I'm not really talented."

"You care about people, and you see potential when others may not. Don't underestimate that. Your brothers were right. You made this show happen and you helped make it even more successful. That's talent."

"I couldn't have done it without you. I don't know if I want to do it without you." The words came out and he didn't regret them. He'd tried not to push. Tried to be subtle and patient in winning her over. But neither were his strong suits. He wanted to be with Kiera, and he had to figure out how to make her see that.

Tapping on the microphone on the stage interrupted his thoughts. "Are y'all ready for another song?" Jessica asked the crowd.

Kiera turned toward the stage and called out,

"Yeah" with everyone else. Tyrone wished he could snatch the microphone away from the curvy singer. Every time he had a chance, something interrupted them.

"Alright, I'll just give you one or maybe two more, then we'll continue to party. That alright?"

Another round of enthusiastic applause went through the small crowd. The music started and Jessica's sultry voice filled the room. Kiera swayed and sang along to the song about love and finding yourself. One verse stuck out to him. A line about not letting someone hold you back and give up your dreams for a false sense of love. Kiera closed her eyes, raised one hand and pressed the other to her heart as she sang. Is that how she felt about him? That he was giving her only a false love? He hadn't promised her forever. He didn't know if he was ready for forever, but he did know he wanted her for the foreseeable future. However long that may be.

He opened his mouth to interrupt her groove and tell her that when her phone buzzed. Her eyes popped open, and she picked it up from her lap. She took one look at the text and her eyes widened.

She grinned up at him and held the phone face out so he could see the screen. "I got the job!"

He looked at the words on the screen and his heart sank. She was going to LA. She'd be gone for weeks. How was he going to convince her of his feelings if she was on the other side of the country?

He looked up into her eyes, bright with excitement and joy, and pushed his own disappointment far down into the pit of his gut. "That's great."

Her smirk said she'd heard the tremor in his voice. "Come on, Tyrone, be happy for me. This is what I need. You know that."

She did need to go to LA. Needed to grow her reputation and career. Needed the money for the hospital bills she had to pay off. Needed to continue to soar. He wanted her to soar and if he wanted to keep her, he'd have to find a way to let her fly while also keep a part of her heart with him.

"I'm very happy for you." He stared into her eyes as he spoke. He meant the words. He couldn't hold her back and keep her from what she wanted. He didn't want Kiera to sacrifice anything because of him. That didn't stop him from feeling as if he was losing her. That she was slipping through his fingers before he'd had the chance to convince her they deserved to give a relationship a try.

Jessica finished her set and thanked the crowd. Tyrone watched as Kiera cheered and waved back at the singer on stage. He wanted to hug her, crush her against him and demand that she change her mind. He wanted to beg and plead for her to stay even though he had no right to hold her from her dreams. He patted his leg and looked around at the happy faces in the room, and resented them being so cheerful when the one thing he wanted he couldn't negotiate his way to having. He needed to move. He was spiraling in a tornado of emotions and he didn't like it, nor did he know how to handle this new feeling. He had to do something and he had to do it now.

He jumped up from the couch. "Wait right here," he said.

Kiera's eyebrows drew together, but a curious smile hovered on her lips. "Um…okay."

He nodded and gave her a thumbs-up. Why he'd done that, he didn't know, but it was either do that with his hands or pull her up with him and hug her like a kid who'd found their favorite lost teddy bear. He hurried out of the VIP section. His brain swirled with the feelings of guilt for wanting to keep her here, frustration knowing he couldn't say that without being an ass, pride to see her achieve what she wanted and another deeper, harder emotion that ached at the thought of not seeing her again.

Towanda took to the microphone on stage. "That was an excellent set. Thank you so much, Jessica!" She clapped and looked at the crowd. "We want to thank everyone here tonight for partying with us at WVOC, your source for hip-hop and R and B. Before we get back to the party, I want to give a few shout-outs to those in the crowd with us." She scanned the crowd, spotted Tyrone and grinned. "First we've got our boy, Tyrone Livingston. WVOC's on-hype man who's now doing big things with his new TV show. Congratulations, Tyrone. Thanks for partying with us."

Tyrone stared up Towanda and a light bulb went off. Did she say shout-out? He grinned and hurried to the stage.

He went over to Towanda and wrapped an arm around her shoulder. "You don't mind if I do a special shout-out do you?"

Towanda's arm slid around his waist. "I don't know, y'all, should we let our boy do a special shout-out?"

The crowd clapped and called out. Towanda handed him the mic. "It's all yours, baby."

He squeezed her in thanks before letting her go. Towanda's arm moved away, but not before her hand lightly grazed his ass. He turned and gave her a come-on-now look but she only smirked and winked. Tyrone shook his head before facing the crowd. He'd have to be sure to let Towanda know they would not be picking up where they'd left off.

"Hey, everyone," Tyrone said into the mic. "Some of y'all may know me. I'm Tyrone Livingston. I used to work for the station and now me and my brothers are the 'Haunted Homeboys' on the Exploration Network." A round of applause and cheers came up from the crowd. Tyrone grinned and nodded. "Cool, glad y'all heard of me. I just want to take a moment to say something. You may not know my girl, Kiera Cox. She the makeup artist on the show and is sitting back in VIP looking absolutely divine. Well, she just found out she got an even bigger job doing makeup on an even bigger show out in LA." A round of applause and cheers interrupted him. "Yeah, I'm very proud of her. I just want to say that in front of all of you. So, raise your glass. To Kiera, you're smart, beautiful and talented. I'm proud of you, baby. Keep on rising to the top."

The crowd clapped for them both. Kiera raised her glass and blew him a kiss. Cameras flashed and the lights from those recording shone from the crowd. This would make the rounds on social media. It would help boost their image and anticipation for the show's premiere. He only hoped this also helped prove to her that he cared. That he would support her move, even if it was killing him inside.

"Aww, that's so sweet," Towanda said after taking back the microphone. "Give it up for my boy, Tyrone and his girl, Kiera." As the crowded cheered again, she whispered to him. "Holla at me when she's out of town."

She turned back to the crowd before he could reply. "Now, let's get this party started. DJ, turn up the music!" Music blasted through the speakers and Towanda danced to the beat.

Tyrone hurried off the stage. He wasn't going to be meeting up with Towanda when Kiera was out of town, but he didn't need to have that conversation here on stage in the middle of the club. He needed a moment to compose himself before going back to Kiera. He hoped the shout-out wasn't too over-the-top. She did say he was impulsive.

He went to the bathroom and when he came out he stopped in his tracks. Cora was standing against the wall next to the bathroom door. Tyrone looked over her shoulder for Sheri or someone else, but the hallway was empty.

Tyrone sighed, exasperated by the thought of having to deal with her. "Excuse me." He tried to walk past her.

She stepped out and blocked his way. "Oh, you real cute and loving with your *girlfriend*, huh."

"I am. Now if you'll let me by." He moved to the side and so did she.

Cora crossed her arms over her chest, pushing up her breasts in the tight, sleeveless black dress she wore. "I know you're not really with her."

Tyrone scowled. "What?"

"I know it," she said smugly. "I overheard you two talking one day during the convention. This little relationship is all a show."

Tyrone's heart raced; how could she possibly know? He and Kiera occasionally talked about their arrangement in public, but they'd kept it to a minimum. If Cora had overheard, why didn't she say anything? No way would he admit to the truth in front of her. Not so she could use his words against him. "I don't know what you're talking about."

She smirked. "Fine. Play dumb. I'm not here to ruin your party."

"Then what are you here for? I know you hate me."

She raised an eyebrow. "Who said I hate you? I mean, yeah, I've got to look out for my cousin, but…" She cocked her head to the side and eyed him with interest. "Li'l Bit told me about how good you were when you two were together. I always wondered if she exaggerated."

"Keep wondering." He moved to go past her, but she put a hand on his chest.

"Why you trying to act like you're some good guy when we both know you're an equal opportunity player?" She reached into her cleavage and pulled out a folded piece of paper. She took the paper and slipped it into the pocket of his pants. "Call me. Show me if you're as good as Li'l Bit said you are."

Someone cleared their throat. He looked up and met Kiera's eyes. Tyrone stepped back. Cora turned, saw Kiera and her smirk widened. She looked back at him. "Now that she has her new job, I'm sure you'll need someone to keep you company."

She pursed her lips at him in a mock kiss before turning and sauntering down the hall. Kiera watched her walk away with hard eyes. Cora waved her hands then continued out of the hall.

Tyrone hurried to Kiera. "It's not what it looks like."

She held up a hand. "You don't owe me an explanation."

Her words and flippant, dismissive words frustrated him more than Cora's weak come-on. "If you pull that we're-not-really-together mess..." He took a stabilizing breath. "Kiera, let me explain."

She shook her head. "Not here. Too many eyes and ears. Smile, take my hand and let's go back out there and have a good time. Neither of us can afford to ruin everything we've built so far."

Chapter Twenty

They stayed at the party for another hour before leaving. Kiera didn't want to talk about what happened with Cora at the club. She'd seen the entire thing. Had headed that way the moment she'd noticed the woman going in that direction after Tyrone got off the stage. Before that, she hadn't known the woman was there, nor would she have cared about her being present. Tyrone and her cousin had ended badly, and she was sticking up for her family. Kiera could respect that, but when she'd smirked at Kiera before following Tyrone, she'd known there would be trouble.

In the car she kept the conversation on the concert and the after party. How much fun she'd had and how much she'd enjoyed seeing Jessica in person.

Anything but Cora's come-on. She wanted to sit in the fantasy a little while longer, despite knowing she couldn't be in a relationship with Tyrone and watch him flirt with women and deal with them propositioning him whenever she wasn't around.

"And thank you for the congratulations on stage," she said. "When you first got up there, I didn't know what you were going to do."

The corner of his mouth lifted in a smile. The streetlights filtering in through the windows cast shadows across his handsome face. "Did you think I was going to embarrass you?"

"Honestly, for a moment I worried you were going to go up there and beg me to stay or something."

"I wouldn't do that to you. I meant what I said. I'm proud of you and even though I'll miss you, I support you."

She stared at the side of his face for several seconds. He finally took his eyes from the road to glance quickly at her. When he raised an eyebrow, she smiled.

"No one's ever really gotten up and cheered for me like that before. It was nice."

"I don't mind cheering for you. Does a part of me wish you'd stay here? Of course. But a bigger part of me wants to see you succeed. I know you've got dreams. I only want to support them the way you've supported me."

When he said things like that, it made it easy to

sink into the fantasy and wrap the dream around her like a blanket. To be honest, he'd started to wear her down. Not by begging or constantly making a case for himself, but by acting like a considerate boyfriend. After he'd gone on stage her defenses weakened. That was until she'd seen the way he'd hugged his coworker, how her hand had accidentally slid across his behind and the quick whispered conversation when they'd passed the microphone. That's when the first cracks in the fantasy appeared tonight. No matter how sweet and loving he was to her, Tyrone was still a casual dating guy who would at least tell her before he slept with someone else.

"I'm sorry about Cora," he said.

Kiera was about to wave away his words and decided against it. She'd wanted to ignore the entire thing. The quick glances he tossed her told her he wasn't going to let her. "You didn't do anything wrong."

He hadn't invited Cora down the hall. Hadn't asked her to sleep with him. Hadn't agreed to call her when Kiera was out of time. She'd cleared her throat before that. She hadn't wanted to hear his answer.

"I didn't expect her to come at me like that," he continued. "I thought she hated me."

"Hate can often be used to disguise someone's true feelings. Feelings they don't want to admit. She's jealous."

"I don't get it. Why would she want to even do that to Li'l Bit?"

"Why does anyone do things they know might hurt the people they're supposed to care about? Selfishness. She wants a piece of you."

The idea made Kiera's skin crawl. She'd wanted to charge down that hall and snatch Cora's hands off Tyrone's body and drag her by her long ponytail down the hall and away from her man. She'd taken a step forward to do so when the truth popped back into her mind. Tyrone wasn't her man and making him her man meant she'd have to deal with those types of situations all the time. It would be her relationship with Mike all over again. That's when the fantasy shattered.

Nothing was more desirable to some women than a reformed playboy. The challenge of proving he hadn't changed was a turn-on for others. She'd have to watch, turn the other cheek, or go with instincts and pull someone by the hair, while hoping Tyrone did his part and turned down any advances. Until the day came when he didn't.

"Well, I don't want a piece of her." He reached over and took her hand in his. "I only want a piece of you."

She smiled despite the cheesy line and shook her head. "Get to the house and you can have a piece of me."

His hand tightened on hers, and his eyes lit up. "You don't have to tell me twice."

Kiera knew she was living dangerously. She'd duct-tape the fractures of the fantasy for the rest of the night. In a few days she would be on her way to LA. Until then she'd take a few snatched moments of fun.

Hadn't she done that from the start? Gone into a fake relationship with Tyrone when she knew she was attracted to him? Slept with him even though she knew doing so would make their situation more complicated? Tried to keep him from her family to avoid connections, but didn't protect herself from caring about his brothers and their girlfriends? She was buried under an avalanche of complicated and messy feelings she wasn't sure she could trust. Something that started as a lie couldn't end well, could it?

She needed space. She needed time to think. She needed to know if this was real or just an illusion created by lust, proximity and mutual benefit.

When they made it home, Kiera didn't give Tyrone time to talk, or for her to think. If he talked, he'd say all the right words, because he'd always know just what to say. She didn't want the right words tonight. She just wanted to be in his arms. To have him make love to her one last time before she did what had to be done to prevent her heart from being broken.

She wrapped her arms around his neck and pulled

his head down to hers. A happy moan rumbled through his chest before he deepened the kiss. He held her tight against him as if he was afraid she'd slip away. Kiera wiggled to loosen his hold. She didn't need affection and tenderness. Not tonight. Tonight, she only needed the physical release. The physical goodbye.

His hands roamed up and down her spine before cupping her behind in a strong grip. Kiera tugged open his shirt. Her fingers played across the muscles of his chest and toyed with the hair there before circling his tight nipple. He sucked in a breath. Burying his nose in her neck, he nipped at the sensitive spot where her neck and shoulder met.

She stepped backward and guided him toward the stairs. Upstairs, they landed on the covers. She expected him to sense her urgency and undress her quickly, but instead he continued to kiss her slowly. His body rubbed against hers. His hands caressed her curves. His tongue played over hers in a slow, sensual glide that made her sex slick. Her hands clutch at his shoulders and arms.

"Tyrone, quit playing with me," she moaned as her back arched for more.

"Who's playing?" he asked in a low, serious voice.

"You know what I want."

His sexy chuckle as he finally released the hooks of her bustier brought out her own grin. "That's what you want?"

She sucked in a breath as the pressure released and her breasts were free. "That and a whole lot more."

She opened her eyes and trailed her finger down his chest, over his abs and to the waistband of his pants. "Make love to me."

The smile left his face. He stared down at her with a look of such need and tenderness her heart ached. He cupped her face and kissed her hard. He removed the rest of her clothes with the same urgency she'd felt before. His soft lips kissed every single inch of skin he revealed. Nipping, licking and sucking until her body squirmed as she clutched the sheets and whimpered in pleasure.

She was lying spread-eagle on the bed, and Tyrone kneeled between her legs, chest heaving with his heavy breaths. His eyes never left hers as slowly rolled the condom down his hard erection. Kiera ran her hands over breasts and stomach. A teasing grin on her face. His nostrils flared. He quickly blanketed her with his body.

Kiera's grin widened. "In a hurry."

"You know what you do to me," he whispered in her ear.

His erection moved heavily against her sex. He rotated his hips, teasing her with the long thick length before pulling back and plunging into her. Filling and stretching her in the most pleasurable way possible. Kiera's nails dug into his back with each deep, rhythmic stroke. The sounds of their ragged breathing and sighs of pleasure filled the room. The heat of his sweat-slickened skin against hers created a sensual friction that vibrated in every nerve of her body. When he rose onto his elbows, caging her in his embrace, he pushed the hair back from her face and he looked down into her eyes.

His expression, one of tenderness and affection, melted the cracks in her defenses. Her eyes prickled with tears as emotions swelled inside her. She was too late. Her heart was already too closely tied to him. She wanted him inside her always, but knew she had to escape. She reached between them and touched herself where they were joined. Her eyes rolled to the back of her head, breaking the hold of his gaze as her body crashed over the edge immediately. Her pleasure always brought him pleasure, and sure enough, his body shuddered, and he gasped as his own orgasm seized him.

He collapsed against her. Kiera smiled contentedly and ran her fingers across his sweat-dampened back. Tyrone lifted his head, got one look at her face and returned her smile.

"You know we can make this work, Kiera," he said before kissing her ear. "Let's make this work."

He didn't play fair. She floated in a haze of pleasure and her heart was coated in the tender emotions that made her want to feel like this forever. Her mouth opened. The word *yes* on the tip of her tongue. His cell phone rang, loud and unwelcome in the middle of their moment.

Swearing, Tyrone pulled away from her. "I'll put it on silence."

She shook her head. "Nah, check it. It's late and could be important."

He moved to the end of the bed and grabbed his discarded pants. Kiera stood and walked toward the door. When he pulled out the phone, he scowled at the screen. "What the…?"

She froze and turned back to him. "Bad news?"

His eyes jerked her way before he shook his head. "No, it's nothing. Looks like someone from the radio station called. It was probably a missed dial." He held up the silent phone. "See, they hung up already."

"You don't need to call back?"

"If it's important they'll leave a message." He darkened his screen then came to her. "Forget that. How about round two in the shower?"

Grinning, Kiera let him follow her to the bathroom. Later, after round two, she was lying on Tyrone's chest and listening to his soft snores while she contemplated what to do next with the feelings she had for him. Light filled the room as his cell phone brightened on the nightstand. She glanced up at him to see if he'd noticed, but he continued to snore. She reached for his phone to darken the screen then paused after seeing a text. A text from Towanda. The former coworker he'd hugged at the station.

Towanda texting wasn't what shoved her out of the warm happy place she'd been in. The words of the message did that. You always come back. Stop playing. I'll see you when she goes to LA.

Chapter Twenty-One

Tyrone hummed to himself as he flipped the last few pancakes on the griddle. He'd gotten up before Kiera and come downstairs after washing up to start breakfast. The smile hadn't left his lips since the first few rays of sunlight came through the window. The night before had been perfect, despite the interaction with Cora. Taking Kiera to see her favorite singer followed by supporting her decision to take the job had been the right moves to make.

He'd seen the look in her eyes. Watched the affirmative nod of her head. She'd finally agreed to stop pretending as if they were still in the fake relationship they'd started months ago. Watching her go to LA would be a heck of a lot easier now knowing the separation wouldn't serve as the start of the "amicable but public breakup" they'd planned.

The sound of Kiera coming down the stairs echoed through the house just as he slid the last of the pancakes onto the stack on the plate next to the griddle. Grinning, he moved the plate of pancakes from the island and took them to the table. There, he'd already set out bacon and sliced fruit he'd prepared earlier, along with orange juice.

"Breakfast is ready," he called out. He turned to the coffee maker and poured coffee into a mug. "I hope you're hungry because I made plenty."

He turned just as she entered the kitchen. She was fully dressed in a stylish tan loungewear suit, her makeup flawless and her hair twisted up. His smile fell as his eyes dropped from her unsmiling face to the suitcase at her side.

"I'm not really hungry," she said in a soft voice.

Tyrone stared at her for a few seconds. His brain tried to process what his eyes saw. She wasn't leaving already, was she? The job wasn't for another week or so. He had more time before he needed to let her go.

"What's going on?"

"I'm going to head back to Atlanta."

"Already?"

She nodded. "Yeah, I need to get some things settled before I go out to LA."

Okay, that made sense. He went back to the table and put down the coffee. "Cool, you can still sit down and eat, and I'll go pack. I'll go with you to Atlanta before you leave."

She shook her head. "That's not necessary."

"It may not be necessary, but that doesn't mean I don't want to go with you."

"But… I don't want you to go with me," she said carefully.

The words hit him with the brutal force of a stun gun, shocking his senses and paralyzing him for several tense seconds. Swallowing hard, Tyrone tried to rein in the hurt ricocheting through his chest. He crossed his arms and tried to sound calm, rational. To not overreact and make things worse. "Why not? I thought that after last night—"

"Last night was just us doing what we do," she said in a detached rush of words. "It didn't mean anything more."

He took a step back. "What? I asked you about us giving this a go. And—"

"And I didn't answer. Your phone rang, remember?"

He scowled as he remembered the interruption. Towanda's call. He forgotten all about her whispered proposition on stage in the aftermath of what happened with Cora. Definitely hadn't expected her to call or send the texts that followed when he didn't answer. Texts once again offering to hook up after Kiera left town. He had no intention of following up Towanda's proposition or letting Kiera know about them.

"Yeah, my phone rang, but that doesn't change how we felt last night. I saw the look in your eyes, and you agreed with me."

She shifted her stance and glanced away. "I had a moment where I thought about what you said, but it was just a moment. That's why I need to go. Before things get even more complicated."

Tyrone hurried to stand in front of her and placed his hands on her shoulders. "Complicated? How? Kiera, we both want this. Why are you fighting this?"

"Are you going to call Towanda when I leave?" she blurted out.

His stomach dropped. The words coming out of her mouth were the last thing he expected to hear. For her to ask the question meant one of two things. "Why are you asking?"

"Because I saw her text last night."

He let go of her shoulders, confusion turning to frustration. "You went through my phone?"

Guilt flashed in her eyes for a half second before she lifted her chin and stared back. "Your phone lit up in the middle of the night and I went to turn it off. Then I saw the text."

"Well, if you saw it then you already know the answer to your question. No, I'm not calling her." Something he'd said in the texts back telling her not to come at him with that anymore.

"But she felt confident enough to send you that message despite us being together. Not only that, but Cora was bold enough to approach you at the after party last night. I mean, damn, Tyrone, how many other women approached you that I don't know about?"

"No one else approached me. And I pushed all of them away. I'm not seeing anyone else. I told you I don't lie about that type of stuff."

"You may not lie, but eventually an offer will come up that you're going to want to follow up. Eventually you're going to be ready to move on."

"You don't know that." She was willing to throw them away over something that might happen in the future? He couldn't believe that was even her excuse right now.

"Do you know if this is forever?"

He closed his eyes and breathed out forcefully through is nose. There she went throwing the word *forever* around. How could he explain that he wasn't ready to promise forever? Not because he only wanted a fling with her, but because the idea of making the promise and not being able to keep it scared the hell out of him. He didn't want to hurt her one day. He only wanted to make her happy for every single day he had her.

He opened his eyes. The stony accusation in her eyes over something he hadn't even done made his defenses rise. "You want me to say I want to get married? I can't. I do want to be with you. Just you. Why can't you get that?" Despite his efforts to try and be calm, the frustration tearing at his insides crept into his voice.

"Why can't you get that I don't want to be in a relationship with a man who has women texting him in the middle of the night about calling her when I'm out of town or coming up to him in the club when we're on a date and asking for sex?" she snapped back. "I don't want to have to turn the other cheek, or worse, show my ass because someone has decided to disrespect me."

"I'll handle that."

"I know you'll try. I know you think you're just being open and honest and doing all the things that you should to avoid being called a jerk. Well, I'm being open and honest, too. I don't want to date the player. Reformed or not. I don't want to have to wonder if someone is smiling in my face and then asking you out when I turn around. I don't want to worry which woman will be the woman to tempt you away. I don't want to become the paranoid girlfriend. I've been there before and it's not fun. I like you, Tyrone, and like I said from the start I want to like you when this ends. That's why I have to start now."

The underlying truth behind her words sliced deep into his chest. "You don't trust me?" The realization punched straight to his insecurities and set them on fire. It wasn't that she didn't believe in them. She didn't believe in him.

"This isn't just about trusting you. This is about

protecting my peace as I try to build my career. Right now, I don't need that in my life."

"No, you don't want *me* in your life. You don't want to believe in me. You think I'll screw this up just like my brothers thought I'd screw everything else up." He no longer tried to hide his frustration, the rising anger. They served to mask the hurt pulsing inside him.

"This isn't about your brothers."

He nodded and rubbed his nose. The pain in his chest grew and unrooted all the things she'd once said. He wasn't a screwup. He wasn't unreliable. All of them had been lies. Lies he'd believed because he'd trusted the sweet words coming out of her mouth. "Nah, it's alright. I get it. You know, you're right. It's best if we follow the plan. I was the one who got things mixed up."

"Tyrone, don't be like that." She reached for him and he stepped back. She didn't follow. She dropped her hand and looked at him with sad but determined eyes. "I need you to understand where I'm coming from."

"I do. I get it. You don't want to deal with the Towandas and Coras in my life. I understand." Didn't want to deal because she didn't trust him to be faithful to her. Couldn't see, or believe, that she was the only woman in his mind, in his heart. "This is for the best. We should just stick with what we planned before emotions get involved. I mean… I don't want my car to get keyed again." He tried to laugh but the sound was thin and hollow.

Kiera winced and sighed. She glanced away before looking back at him. "Look, I'll continue to post some of the selfies we took and then phase it down to shots of me working in LA. If you do the same then we can release a statement right after the show premieres. It won't be a big deal, and everyone will understand. You'll just have to…" Her voice trailed away.

His chin shot up. "Have to what?" He didn't want to hear it, but he already knew what she was going to say.

She shifted from foot to foot, then quickly said, "You'll just have to not be seen with other women while I'm gone."

The words were a slap in the face. She really did think he was going to screw everything up. That he'd go this far, tell her he wanted her, but still turn to another woman when she walked away. He took a step back. "Don't worry. I'll be sure anything I do stays off the radar." The words were ambiguous and mean. He was lashing out and even though he wanted to pull her into his arms and beg her to stay, to trust him, to believe in him, pride closed his throat.

She sucked in a breath and raised her chin. "Good to know." After one last glance at the table, she focused back on him. "I'll text you when I get to Atlanta. Thanks again for the concert last night. It was cool."

"No problem. I just called in a favor at the station. It wasn't a big deal." The lie was like sandpaper in his throat. Last night had been a big deal for him, but he'd already given her more of him than she wanted. He wasn't giving her more.

Disappointment clouded her eyes before she nodded. "Goodbye, Tyrone." She turned and walked out. With each echo of her footsteps, the anger, frustration and pain inside him swelled and pressed against the walls of his throat until he thought he'd choke on them. The door opened and quietly closed. The bubble of his emotions burst. Tyrone turned to the table and shoved the stack of pancakes onto the floor.

Chapter Twenty-Two

Instead of going back to her apartment, Kiera went straight to her parents' house in east Atlanta. Sunday afternoons in the fall at her parents' home meant football and lots of food. Both of her parents were huge Atlanta Falcons fans, and football season was the only time during the year when they attended the 8:00 a.m. church service versus the 11:00 a.m. service in order to get home in time to enjoy the afternoon games.

"Why didn't you bring Tyrone?" The question was the first thing her mom said immediately after hugging and kissing Kiera.

Kiera just barely avoided rolling her eyes though she couldn't suppress a sigh. "Good to see you, too, Mom."

Evie Cox laughed and shook her head. She was Kiera's height, with cocoa skin, a wide smile and cinnamon-brown hair thanks to the home coloring kit she wouldn't give up no matter how much Kiera tried to convince her to go to a professional stylist. Her mom wore her favorite Falcons jersey with a pair of black joggers.

"You know I'm happy to see you," her mom said. "I'd just like to also meet the guy you're dating."

"When it's time I'll let you know," Kiera said looking over her mom's shoulder and breathing in the scents filling the house. "I'm so hungry. What smells so good?"

Mentioning being hungry was enough to put Evie into "mommy" mode and she immediately ushered Kiera to the kitchen. Her brother, Rodrick, and his girlfriend, Contessa, were there along with their two-year-old son. Kiera went over to her dad, who was sitting in his spot in front of the television, and kissed his cheek. Silas Cox matched his wife with his own Falcons jersey and black joggers, except his short, salt-and-pepper afro was covered by the Falcons hat she'd gotten him for Christmas the year before. Her dad's best friend and next-door neighbor, Walter, was also there. He'd claimed a spot on one of the couches and waved a hand while giving her a welcoming, gap-toothed smile.

Kiera helped her mom get the paper plates and cups ready before her dad blessed the food. After everyone filled their plates and settled around the living room to eat and watch the game, Kiera finally relaxed. This is what she needed. Time away to clear her head and think. She'd spent so much time wrapped up in the fantasy she'd created with Tyrone that she'd started to believe it.

The look on his face had haunted her on the ride back to Atlanta. The look of disappointment and hurt when she said she didn't want to deal with the drama that came with being in a relationship with him. Tyrone wasn't the playboy or womanizer he'd been accused of being, or the screwup he believed himself to be. She knew that. He wouldn't intentionally hurt her, but she also believed one day he'd walk away and be with another woman, leaving her heart crushed.

She loved him. She knew that, but the love was new and growing and she hadn't allowed it to settle in and take root. If she'd stayed she would never be able to untangle herself without suffering. Heartbreak and pain were distractions she couldn't afford while she built her brand and crawled her way out of debt. No, walking away was the best thing for them both. The ache now would heal a lot faster than it would six months to a year from now, when he'd ultimately cut things off.

"Hey, Kiera, isn't that your boy?" Contessa asked and pointed at the television.

Kiera looked up from her phone to the screen. Her dad scrolled during commercials and stopped on a promo for the new season of *Haunted Homeboys*. The sight of Tyrone with his sexy smile and teasing eyes made her heart clench.

"Yeah…that's him."

Her dad slapped his thigh. "Why don't you bring him around? I need to make sure he's good enough for my baby girl."

Kiera played with the mac and cheese on her plate. "I'm figuring that out, too, Dad. When I know, you'll meet him."

Walter narrowed his eyes on her. "Why wouldn't he be good enough? Haven't ya'll been dating for a while? You don't know yet?"

Her dad pushed Walter's shoulder. "Leave my girl alone."

"Thanks, Daddy," Kiera said.

Silas shot her with an inquisitive look. "Even though I'm wondering the same thing myself. He's not treating you bad or anything, is he?"

Kiera shook her head. "No. He's good."

"I heard he was ho," Contessa said while wiping smeared mashed potatoes from her son's face.

Her brother nudged her. "Don't say that?" He looked at Kiera. "But for real. Is he? He stepping out on you?"

Kiera pressed a hand to her temple. Why had she thought coming home was a good idea? "No. He's not stepping out and he's not a ho."

"Your daddy was a ho," her mom said from her recliner next to her husband.

"Momma!" Kiera exclaimed.

Evie shrugged and continued to eat her food. "What?" She looked at her husband. "Am I lying?"

Her dad waved a hand. "I dated around."

Her mom rolled her eyes. "You were a ho. Don't clean it up for the kids. When we first met your dad was just playing around with me."

Kiera's eyes swung to her father. "Daddy? For real?"

"Why you gotta say it like that, Evie?" he said, sounding petulant.

"Because it's true. I wasn't too worried because I knew you were a ho, so I didn't put much stock into the sweet words you were saying."

Her brother put a hand to his forehead. "Wait, Momma, don't talk like that."

Kiera laughed and pointed at her brother. "What's the matter? Momma needed love, too."

"That don't mean I wanted to hear about it," Rodrick grumbled and did an exaggerated shudder.

"Yeah, your mom didn't think I was serious when I tried to talk to her," her dad said. "It took her a while to realize I wasn't playing around."

"Sure did," Evie said, calmly taking another bite of her mac and cheese.

Kiera looked from her mom to her dad. They'd talked about how they'd met through mutual friends, and that they hadn't immediately hit it off before falling in love, but this was the first time they'd gotten into the trials before their triumphs. "When did you know he wasn't playing around?" Kiera asked.

Her mom sighed then smiled. "It was the little things. He started backing up the promises he would make. Showing up when he said he would. Pushing aside all the little hoochie mommas that kept trying to tempt him."

Silas scoffed. "They weren't all hoochie mommas."

Walter laughed so hard he almost spit out his beer. "Don't lie, Silas. I knew you back then. Some of them were hoochie mommas."

Her dad glared at his friend while Kiera and her brother stared back, stunned. Contessa laughed along with her mother. They were obviously tickled by this tidbit of information.

"Whatever, Silas," her mom said. "You had women always trying to approach you. Especially after we went public. Oh, them old girlfriends tried hard to snatch him back."

Contessa wrinkled up her nose. "And you were okay with that? I be trying to fight any woman who come for my man." She reached over and patted Rodrick's shoulder.

Kiera took a bite of chicken to avoid responding. Contessa's short fuse and her brother's lingering exes had led to most of the drama in their relationship. She knew her brother loved Contessa and, heaven help her, Contessa was crazy for her brother, but Kiera didn't want any relationship resembling theirs.

"It was annoying," her mom admitted. "But I knew that it was also a test. If he slipped up one time—" her mom snapped her fingers "—then I was gone. A person is gonna do what they want to do. I don't believe in this a-man-is-just-a-man nonsense. If you care, then you show you care. If you don't, then you do whatever you want without regard to the other person. He cared. Once we were together, he didn't slip up. And that's all I needed."

Later, when Kiera was alone with her mom in the kitchen to get a slice of the lemon pound cake she'd made, Kiera asked, "Momma, what you said earlier about you and Daddy. Was that true?"

"Why would I lie?" Her mom paused in slicing the cake and putting in onto paper plates.

"I mean…didn't you wonder? If you were making the right decision to trust him or not?"

Her mom watched her for a second. Kiera squirmed, getting the feeling that her mom immediately understood the reasons behind the question.

Evie went back to slicing the cake. "I did. Back then I didn't know that we'd get married, have you and your brother and build a life together. I just knew that, despite his faults, I was crazy about him. As long as he respected me, I stuck with him. We went day by day."

Kiera toyed with the edge of the plastic bag holding the paper plates. "That's a lot of faith to put into a relationship that may go nowhere."

"Any relationship can end up going nowhere. It doesn't matter if it's love at first sight, falling in love with a person years after meeting them, or just deciding to play around. Some relationships stick, others don't. If you choose to be with someone and they're treating you right, enjoy the time you have with them because tomorrow isn't promised. No matter how perfect that person may or may not be."

Kiera sighed. "That's not very reassuring."

Her mom placed a hand over Kiera's. Kiera looked up from the plastic bag into her mother's knowing smile. "You want me to give you a fairy tale and tell you everything will be okay? I can't do that, baby. That's for you to decide and learn on your own. If he makes you happy and treats you right, then you have to decide if that's enough. If it's not, oh, well. Don't hide behind excuses or try to make sense of why you do or don't want something. You know what you want."

"But I don't know if I should want…him."

Her mom patted her hand. "Aren't you going to LA?" Kiera nodded and her mom shrugged. "Well, guess you'll have plenty of time to figure that out."

Chapter Twenty-Three

The smell of waffles, fried food and coffee greeted Tyrone as he walked through the doors of the Waffle House in Sunshine Beach. He didn't frequent the Waffle House. One, he preferred pancakes, and two, he wasn't particularly welcome there. His eyes met Li'l Bit's from across the room. The "welcome to Waffle House" greeting had barely crossed her lips before her smile faded to one of annoyance.

He'd come in on a Wednesday afternoon hoping it wouldn't be as crowded as it typically was during the morning shift or on a weekend. Based on the crowded booths and the counter, he'd clearly assumed wrong. He made his way to the only open seat at the end of the bar. Li'l Bit and one other waitress were working along with the two cooks on the grills.

He gave her a tight smile and raised a hand, hoping it would lure her over to him. She rolled her eyes and looked away.

"Kerry, can you get the guy at the end of the bar?" she called to the other waitress.

Kerry shook her head. "Nah, Sheri, don't think because it's your last day that you get to put off the work. I'm about to serve my table, anyway." Despite her refusal, Kerry grinned at Li'l Bit with the words.

Shaking her head, Sheri finally came over to Tyrone. "How can I help you?"

He pointed to the plastic tiara with the word *Congratulations* spelled out in purple letters on her head. "What's with the crown?"

"Huh?" She reached for her head. "Oh, I forgot I was wearing that." She glanced away as if embarrassed, but didn't pull it off her head. "Do you want something to drink?"

"Nah, I was hoping I'd get a chance to talk to you."

Her eyes narrowed. "For what?"

"I just…need to talk to you. That's all."

She glanced around the crowded room. "Well, we're busy right now, so I can't talk. If that's all you want, then don't hold up a seat." She turned to walk away.

"Let me get an orange juice," he said before she could escape.

She turned back to him with a scowl. "Is that all?"

"And a waffle…and some bacon and eggs."

She huffed as if not happy but wrote down his order. "Coming right up." Her words had not been spoken with a smile.

Tyrone couldn't blame her. They hadn't been on speaking terms in years. He didn't know how else to talk to her. They'd both changed their numbers since their disastrous time together. He wasn't about to ask around town for her number and there was no way he would just show up at her home, either. Coming to her job wasn't ideal, but it was the best he had.

She brought back his orange juice and then his food. Tyrone ate slowly and waited as the other patrons finished their meals, paid and left. It didn't take long to understand why there was a crowd or the reason for her congratulatory tiara. He overheard enough of the conversations to realize that many of the people were her regular customers coming to an impromptu farewell party. She was opening her own restaurant and today was her last day working here.

By the time the restaurant was clear and only he and one other person remained, he asked her again, "Can you talk now?"

Sighing, she tapped the ticket in front of him with a manicured finger. "Pay this and then we'll talk."

He picked up the receipt, pulled cash out of his wallet and handed it over to her. "Keep the change."

"Don't worry, I will," she said, going to the register.

Tyrone stood and followed her to the register. "Now can we talk?"

Sighing, she turned to Kerry and the cooks. "I'm taking ten."

"Don't make it fifteen just because it's your last day," Kerry teased again.

"Believe me, this won't take long."

Sheri came around the counter and went out the front door without looking back at Tyrone. He hurried to follow. She walked to the end of the building, away from the front door but not shielded from the sight of anyone who might enter. She crossed her arms over her chest and cocked her head to the side.

"Speak."

Tyrone bit the inside of his jaw. Forty-five minutes of waiting and eating a meal he didn't want, and his patience was thin. But he was trying to be a better person. A person people could rely on and not expect to ruin everything. He took a fortifying breath and met her eyes.

"I'm sorry," he said in a rush.

"For what?"

He looked at her as if she'd lost her mind. "For what happened." When she continued to look confused, he continued. "Between us. I'm sorry for hurting you."

She blinked and her head shot back. "Hold up. Are you apologizing for that?"

"Yeah. I thought we were on the same page, but

obviously we weren't. I hurt your feelings. It wasn't intentional, but that's no excuse. So, I'm sorry."

Step one in being a better person was acknowledging your faults. Step two was trying to make amends for the people he'd hurt. Or at least that was some of the advice he'd gotten online when he'd searched for how to get your woman back. He didn't want Sheri, but he did want to prove to Kiera that he wasn't unreliable or untrustworthy. She'd recommended he clear the air with Li'l Bit, so that's what he was doing.

Sheri held up a hand. "Stop. You don't need to apologize."

"Yes, I do."

She shook her head. "No, you don't. If anyone should apologize…" She rubbed the back of her neck before flipping her hair over her shoulder and shifting from one foot to the other. "It should be me," she mumbled.

This time he did a double take. He turned his head and leaned his ear closer. "Hold up. What did you say?"

Her eyes narrowed but she answered. "I said it should be me. I shouldn't have keyed your car. You were up front and open. I knew we were done when I saw you with that woman."

He placed his hands on his hips. "Then why did you key my car?"

"Because I was mad and in a bad head space. Then

Cora started talking all kinds of trash and there might have been tequila shots involved…" She glanced away, then huffed out, "I'm sorry."

"If you're sorry then why have you been hating on me for so long?"

"I haven't been hating on you." When he raised his eyebrows, she waved a hand. "Alright, a little, but I had to on principle. Plus, I was embarrassed. I don't like acting out like that and now everyone in town knows and is waiting on me to be all dramatic around you. So, I ignore you."

Her words were true. Their breakup followed by her keying his car had been the talk of Sunshine Beach for weeks. It was still brought up whenever the two of them were in a room together. Everyone would wait for one of them to show out. He'd tried ignoring her for the same reason.

"How about we're both sorry then?" he said.

"Why are you apologizing, anyway? Are you in some ten-step program or something?"

He shook his head. "Nah, it's just…someone said maybe I should apologize."

A knowing smile spread across her lips. "Your girlfriend."

The mention of Kiera sent a pain through his chest. He rubbed the ache as if the movement would make the pain go away. It did not. "Yeah."

"I heard she went to LA for a job," she said.

He nodded. "She did."

"Are you going to go out there after her?"

"Huh?"

Sheri looked at him as if he was stupid. He was used to that, but this time he didn't understand why. "It's obvious that you care about her. I thought you'd be running out there to be with her."

"About that…" He wasn't sure how much to say. Had Cora spilled the beans about his relationship with Kiera being fake?

Sheri flicked her wrist before he could finish. "I don't care what Cora said about you two being fake. You really liked her. I could tell."

His eyebrows drew together. "How could you tell?"

"The little things. I mean, we hooked up, but you never really paid attention to me. You were always focused on her. It was different. I didn't believe you'd ever fall, but I was wrong."

"I do like her. A lot." Sheri's words only frustrated him more. If Sheri could see it then why couldn't Kiera? Did she really trust him so little?

"So, what's the problem?"

He thought about keeping things to himself, but since she'd been honest with him and apologized, and honestly he needed a woman's opinion, he spilled his guts. He told her about what happened at the club and what her cousin had done.

Li'l Bit rolled her eyes and pressed her fingers to

her temple after he told her about Cora's proposition. "No, she didn't."

"You don't sound surprised?"

"I'm not," she said with an eye roll. "She was into you back when we were hooking up. I knew she would jump on a chance with you. Honestly, I was glad to see you weren't that dirty."

"I wouldn't do that." Messing with the friends and family members of a woman he slept with was a recipe for disaster.

"I know, but she tries hard. I'll deal with her later. If you really want your girl back, then you focus on what you can do to prove to her that you two belong together and forget everyone trying to come between y'all. That's what matters."

"Yeah, well, I don't know if it's that easy. My reputation doesn't help." His eyes narrowed. "You didn't start any rumors about me?"

"No. I was mad, but I didn't care enough to start rumors." She lifted a shoulder. "Cora, on the other hand, showed me the online account that first posted those accusations about you being a dog and playing women."

"Did she create the account?"

Her gaze slid away and she scratched the back of her head. "I don't think she would."

"If she did, will you tell her to stop?"

"I don't know if it's her, but if it is…then, yeah. I'll tell her to stop."

"Thank you." He doubted the two of them would ever be great friends, but after this talk, he felt like a load had been lifted. The tension between them and the expectation of drama whenever they were in a room had been one of the reasons he'd been so anxious to leave Sunshine Beach. Now that the air was clear, neither of them would have that lingering over them. Kiera had been right—talking to Li'l Bit and clearing the air was the right thing to do.

Sheri looked at her watch. "My break is about over."

"No problem. Thanks for taking the time to talk to me."

She shrugged and went to the door. She stopped and looked back. "And, for what it's worth, I think you should go after her. Fight for her. I haven't met a woman who doesn't appreciate it when her man fights for her."

He nodded but didn't say anything as she went back inside. Tyrone considered her words as he walked to his car. He did want to fight for Kiera, but would she want or appreciate that? She didn't trust him and he didn't believe chasing her across country to beg her to believe him would work. The right words didn't always restore or create trust. He'd have to find a way to show her. He wasn't sure how, or if he could combat her doubts about him. Even worse, he was afraid of fighting for her only to lose the battle. What if she was right and he was looking at them through the safety of a fake relationship with no emotional stakes? For now, maybe they both needed space to figure things out.

Chapter Twenty-Four

Tyrone looked at the social-media notification on his phone and his stomach dropped. Kiera had updated her page and the joint statement they'd agreed on announcing their breakup was the first thing he saw. He wished she hadn't tagged him in it, but that was the other part they'd agreed on. That they would tag each other to further prove that their breakup was amicable, and due to months apart caused by their busy schedules.

The months of separation hadn't eased the ache in his chest. Her job in LA had turned into another job in New York. She'd returned to Atlanta briefly before going back out to LA to work on a television show. During the entire separation, they'd kept up appearances as much as they could with a "long-distance" relationship. They'd tagged each other on social-media posts about missing the other and live-chatted with the viewers after the premiere of *Haunted Homeboys*.

> Although Tyrone and I were both committed to making things work, the truth is our schedules have kept us apart more than together. The decision to break up wasn't an easy one, but it was the best for us at this time.

He read the words and wanted to throw his phone across the room.

"What's wrong with you?" Wes's voice broke into his thoughts.

Tyrone looked up from his phone at his brothers sitting around the living area in their family home. They'd met up over the weekend to do some yard work and maintenance. Now that the work was done, they'd decided to catch up on the basketball games and celebrate the renewal of a third season with pizza, wings and beer.

Tyrone wanted to ignore the announcement. To pretend as if it was a hallucination and that he'd be able to call up Kiera tomorrow and she'd say she'd changed her mind and missed him as much as he missed her, but he couldn't. Not only did his brothers and their partners follow Kiera on social media, but people at the network and many of his friends also did.

He held up his phone. "Kiera announced our breakup."

Wes sat up straight. "Wait, what?"

Dion scowled. "You two broke up? When? I thought you said things were good even though she was out of town."

Tyrone took a long breath. He'd kept the truth from them for so long that a part of him wanted to continue to lie. A bigger part of him wanted to be honest. He'd kept this in for too long. The doubt about giving her space. The yearning for her that had grown with each day. The frustration of only talking to her via texts or quick phone calls to strategize on the slow demise of their relationship. He'd thought he would get over things, but he hadn't. He loved her. Missed her. And he didn't know what to do.

"We both agreed to announce the breakup," he said.

"Why? What happened?" Dion asked.

Tyrone steeled himself and then told the truth. "We were never really together."

The dual exclamation of "what" by his brothers was followed by multiple demands for an explanation. Tyrone spilled the entire truth. To their credit, they didn't interrupt or go off as he explained. Wes looked shell-shocked while disappointment filled Dion's eyes.

"Go ahead and say it," Tyrone said when he was done. "Say that I messed up and that I could have ruined everything."

Dion shook his head. "That's not what I was going to say."

"Then what were you going to say? I can see the look on your face. 'Tyrone screwed up again.'"

"You done speaking for me?" Dion said, his voice getting irritated.

Wes held up a hand. "Chill, Dion, let's hear why he thought he couldn't tell us, his brothers, the only family he has left, the two people who will always be there for him, about the situation with Kiera."

"That's why," Tyrone exclaimed. "Because y'all would judge me. You'd think I was going to ruin everything like I did when we were younger."

"No," Dion said slowly before meeting Tyrone's eyes. "Your idea was smart. The fact that you got Kiera to go along with it for so long is even more of a shock."

Tyrone blinked. "You think my idea was smart?"

"Yeah, the network was considering letting us go. You settling down so to speak fed in to their family-friendly image. I get why you did it, but you didn't have to keep things from us. We would have understood."

Wes lifted a shoulder. "We might have given you a hard time because that's what we do, but we would've been okay."

Tyrone stared at his brothers. He'd expected accusations of him being impulsive or claims that his actions were proof of his continued irresponsibility. Not for them to…agree with his decision. "It was my fault that the show almost didn't get renewed. I felt it was my job to fix things."

Dion looked at Tyrone as if he'd uttered the dumbest phrase he'd ever heard. "You're not in this alone, Tyrone. We're brothers. Yeah, we're going to argue and disagree sometimes, but that doesn't mean you have to fix things on your own. If we have a problem, we'll all figure it out. Understand?"

The steel in his brother's voice would usually make Tyrone bristle. He typically hated when Dion went into "Dad mode" on them. Today, the reassurance of his older brother brought forth another emotion. Appreciation.

Tyrone nodded. "I get it."

Dion gave a stiff nod. "Good." He picked up his beer and took a long swallow.

"Dang, man," Wes said. "I really thought you two were together. You seemed to really be into her."

"I was. I am." Tyrone pushed away the plate with his slice of pizza. He was no longer hungry.

"Then why don't you tell her?" Wes asked.

"I did. She didn't want to go from fake relationship to real relationship. She said she didn't want to deal with the women hitting on me and having to pretend as if she was okay. Then she said one day I would be ready to move on and she didn't want to end up like Li'l Bit and key my car."

Dion cringed. "Damn. That's tough."

"Tell me about it."

"Look, I can't tell you if you and Kiera belong together or will be together forever or not," Dion said. "I wasn't sure if things would work out when Vanessa left, but I knew I had to at least give us a try. That's why I took a job to be near her."

"You telling me to move to Atlanta or follow her to LA?" Tyrone asked sitting up straight. Had Li'l Bit's advice from months ago been right? Had he wasted all this time by not following her?

His brother held up a hand in a hold-on fashion. "No, what I'm saying is that if things are meant to be then fate will have a way of pulling you two together."

Tyrone didn't want to hear about fate. If things continued as they were, then Kiera would move farther and farther away from him. Seeing the statement, reading the finality in the words, poked at the impulsive side he'd ignored in his quest to prove his trustworthiness. "Li'l Bit said I should fight for her."

Wes held up a hand. "Hold up. Why you talking to her about Kiera?"

"Because I went to apologize to her about what happened between us. It was right before she opened her new restaurant."

Wes's eyes nearly popped out of his head. "You apologized? What brought on that level of maturity?"

"Kiera," Tyrone admitted. "She thought it would help and it did. Li'l Bit said women want their men to fight for them and that's what I thought you were saying."

"There's a fine line between fighting for a woman and harassing her," Dion cautioned, sounding every bit like the responsible older brother. "If she says she's not interested then listen to what she says." Tyrone's shoulders slumped in disappointment. "But," Dion continued, "if you *happen* to be in the same place as her, and if you two *happen* to talk, and if the spark that was in her eye when you two were pretending to date *happens* to come back, then I suggest you be truthful with her. Tell her how you feel. Tell her that you're willing to do whatever it takes to prove to her your love is real. Don't leave everything up to fate. You gotta put in some effort, too."

Chapter Twenty-Five

Kiera arrived fashionably late at Sofia Gomez and Tanner Logan's anniversary party. Much like their wedding a year before, they'd held it at the same venue and asked the network to hire people to fill in the gaps as they celebrated their anniversary. Though Kiera didn't need the money from working as a professional seat filler, when the network contacted her and asked her to come with a plus-one, she'd accepted for old times' sake. She was not attending because she hoped Tyrone might also be there. She enjoyed a good party and good food. This would be both.

"How much am I getting paid for this?"

Kiera had shown up to the party not only looking good in a black-and-red-lace, off-the-shoulder dress that hugged her curves and stopped just above the knees, but she'd also come on the arm of one of the most handsome men she knew, her cousin Terrence. Tall, with toasted caramel skin, chocolate-brown eyes and a low fade that was sharper than a scalpel, her first cousin would have received a certification in pretty boy if there was one available. He looked amazing in a dark suit and matching shirt.

If she might run into her ex-boyfriend, real or not, then she couldn't show up without a lifeline.

Terrence agreed to come not out of the goodness of his heart, but because of the promise of payment. She'd agreed to give him half of the payment for being a seat filler. That, and he'd served as her buffer between her good sense and her heart where an ex was concerned before. She'd done the same for him in the past, too.

"You're getting paid enough," she told him. "Now just be charming and don't make me look bad."

"How in the world could I possibly make you look bad?" Terrence said, rubbing his chin and giving his I-know-I-look-good smile.

Kiera rolled her eyes and shook her head. "By opening your mouth and saying something embarrassing about me. Remember here, I am a glamorous and popular makeup artist. Not the ugly teenager I used to be."

Terrence nudged her shoulder. "Stop that. You

went through an awkward phase. We all did. Quit calling yourself ugly."

She smiled appreciating his pep talk. "I'm far from ugly now."

He grinned. "That's what I'm talking about. Now, where is the bar?"

"Let's greet the happy couple first. We only have to stay long enough for them to get some pictures of the crowd and make a speech. Once that's done, the promo stuff is over and we can leave. And remember—"

"If I see you talking to that Tyrone guy come and save you from yourself," he answered, deadpan.

"Why you gotta say it like that?"

"Because, you obviously like the guy. Why are you trying to avoid him? There wasn't a really good reason to break up with him."

She hadn't told her family about the fake relationship. She'd decided that since she and Tyrone were separated because of work, then there was no reason to get her family involved. Plus, they'd worry about her and the lengths she'd go through to try to climb out of debt. Her parents struggled hard enough to make ends meet. She didn't want them making themselves strapped by trying to send her money.

"We just drifted apart. Besides, he's probably dating someone else by now. I'm not about to make a fool of myself by chasing after a guy."

"Whatever you say."

"Just come on."

She led Terrence toward Sofia and Tanner. She hadn't seen Tyrone on the arm of another woman in their time apart, but he had promised her that he wouldn't play in to the rumors or embarrass her even when they were separated. He was probably glad that their fake relationship was officially over. He hadn't released his statement, but they'd agreed to post them. Maybe he was too busy getting back out in the dating scene to worry about getting a breakup post on his account.

Or, maybe he misses you, too.

The hopeful thought had teased her in the days since she posted the statement with no response from him. His social-media accounts were all silent. No updates, no pictures, nothing. Online gossips speculated that he was tending to a broken heart. Kiera didn't want to admit to how much she hoped he was as miserable without her as she felt without him, then immediately felt silly for wishing misery on a man who hadn't disagreed with any of her public breakup plans over the past few months. Tyrone had moved on. The faster she accepted that, the better.

They greeted the hosts and then mingled with the rest of the guests. Cameras captured everyone laughing, dancing and toasting to the happy couple. Kiera didn't see Tyrone anywhere in the crowd. She'd worried for nothing. He was one of the network's stars now. He didn't need to attend parties for Sofia and

Tanner to get recognition or fame. He and his brothers had their own following now.

She left Terrence at the bar and went to the food table to grab a piece of cake. Maybe the sugary treat would lift her mood. She was even more silly for being disappointed that he wasn't there. The dancing had started, and the music pumped through the ballroom. She'd typically be out on the dance floor. She remembered the wedding. Dancing with Tyrone and the kiss that had ignited everything. She'd laughed and felt so much promise and excitement that night. Tonight was nothing like that.

She accepted the slice of cake from the server cutting and handing out slices. She put a large spoonful of the delicious dessert into her mouth and turned to go back to the bar when her eyes collided with Tyrone's.

He'd been behind her. Not close enough to block her, but close enough that she couldn't pretend she hadn't seen him. He looked as handsome and tempting as ever in a dark burgundy suit with a black button-up shirt open at the collar. Her gave her the crooked smile that made her heart clutch before closing the distance between them.

"Is the cake any good?"

She swallowed the lump of cake and sucked in a breath. His cologne and the recognizable scent that was unique to him invaded her senses. Kiera licked her lips quickly. "Yeah...it's really sweet."

"I was looking around the party for you." His gaze, intent and laser-focused, remained on her. His eyes drifted over her face as if he was committing her to memory.

"Oh, really?" Her voice was shaky.

"Yeah, I wasn't sure if you'd be here tonight. I'd hoped you would be."

Her heart fluttered against her chest. She cleared her throat and tried to calm down. To not show just how desperate she felt to have his arms around her again. "How've you been?"

He gave a casual shrug. "Pretty good. Our show got renewed for a third season."

"I heard. That's great."

The news should have made his face light up. That's all he'd wanted—for the show to be successful. Instead, he stared back at her as if searching for something infinitely more important.

"How about you?" he asked. "Are you going back to LA?"

She shook her head. "No, I actually got a standing position as lead makeup artist at Park Studios. I get a steady paycheck and I can stay in Atlanta."

His eyes lit up. His shoulders relaxed. "That's great. Congratulations."

"I know. I finally paid off my medical bills and can comfortably afford my almost too expensive apartment."

He chuckled. "It's a nice place."

"It is a nice place."

They stood there awkwardly for a moment. Kiera searched for something to say other than "I'm sorry. I changed my mind. I want to be with you." But the words stuck in her throat. She'd turned him down and been insistent about it six months before. He'd probably moved on. Probably had a date with him.

"Did you come alone?" she asked, worried he'd hear the hope in her voice.

"I did. I'm not seeing anyone."

Her speeding heart raced even more. "Oh. Are you…just getting back out there after our announcement? I bet you're glad that's over. Now you can finally start living it up again, huh." She tried to laugh but it sounded weird and forced so she took another bite of cake.

"You know I'm not glad it's over," he said seriously. "I miss you, Kiera. The stuff I said six months ago. It still stands."

She froze. The bite of cake turned to cement in her mouth, sealing her lips as his words bounced around her head. Was he serious? Did he still feel the way he'd felt before? Was she ready to move forward?

Hell yes, you are! Didn't you dream about this man every day since you parted?

A hand brushed her shoulder. "Kiera, the toasts and stuff are over. Let's get out of here."

Kiera turned toward Terrence. She widened her eyes at her cousin. Now! He was really coming now!

Kiera forced the bite of cake in her mouth down her throat and tipped her head toward the door. She prayed he understood her body language. He needed to get lost.

Terrence shook his head. "Come on. Let's go." He glanced at Tyrone and lifted his chin, then took Kiera's wrist, her hand still holding the cake plate, and pulled her toward the door.

Kiera glanced over her shoulder at Tyrone's confused face. She was finally able to form words as he pulled her away from Tyrone. "What are you doing?"

Terrence gave her a pitiful look. "Saving you from yourself."

"I don't want to be saved." She wanted to run back and fling herself in Tyrone's arms.

Terrence continued to pull her until they were outside of the party. "Yes, you do. Make him work for it at least, cuzzo. I could tell from the moment you saw him that you were lost."

The words stopped her in her tracks. She cringed. "Was I that bad?"

"Hell yeah. If he really wants you, he'll come after you."

"No, he won't. He has his choice of women."

"If he doesn't and it's really like that then you deserve better, anyway," Terrence said easily. The statement was both blunt and true. "Now, let's go. This party is boring and I'm ready to catch the end of the fight. Rodrick and Contessa texted that they're heading to your place to watch now."

Sighing, Kiera took another bite of the cake. Terrence was right. She had been about to jump into Tyrone's arms and say she made a mistake. Now that she was out of his presence, she wondered if doing that would have been a grand romantic gesture, or just her being silly and desperate.

Call him tomorrow. Take twenty-four hours.

Nodding, she followed Terrence to his car. She'd call him tomorrow. Jumping into Tyrone's arms twenty-four hours after he said he wanted to try again was better than immediately. She tried to reassure herself with those words as she slipped into the passenger side of her cousin's car.

Tyrone couldn't believe she'd walked off. With another guy. He'd said he still felt the same as he did six months ago, and she'd just walked off. With another guy. She'd smiled at him and looked at him with those beautiful eyes while wearing that sexy dress, then given him an apologetic smile before walking off. With another guy!

The memory pounded through his brain over and over. It taunted him as he got sympathetic looks from mutual friends after she left the party. Teased him as he said his goodbyes and went to his car. Terrorized him with the fear that she had indeed moved on.

"Of course, she moved on. She was with another dude!" he exclaimed into the silent interior of his car.

He'd tried to listen to Dion. To let fate bring them back together and see if they were truly meant to be. Except he'd decided to help fate out a little bit. The moment he'd heard about the anniversary party, he'd thought of Kiera, how they'd met, and RSVP'd with the hope that maybe she'd be there, too. It was the fifth Exploration Network event he'd attended to try and help fate. He'd finally found her. And she'd left. With another man.

He shook his head and his hands tightened on the steering wheel. He'd left the party and decided to go back to his hotel room. He should just give up. That's exactly what the jealous, angry voice in his head told him. That voice said he should let this go. Get back out there. End six months of celibacy with someone who wasn't leaving parties with another guy.

His heart, that sensitive organ that hadn't felt right since she walked away, whispered that he had a chance. Murmured that he should remember the bright light that came to her eyes. The way she'd leaned toward him. The half second before that dude walked up and she'd looked as if she was going to step into Tyrone's arms. His heart believed what he'd seen wasn't wishful thinking or an illusion.

Maybe that's why he ultimately ended up parking in front of her apartment building instead of going to the hotel. With every step he took toward her door, reason screamed at him to turn around. To go back if he wasn't prepared to handle what he found. Finding her with that guy and having her kick him out of her apartment would hurt him more than just watching her walk away. But the sliver of hope, wrapped up in the love he felt for her, drove his steps. If he hadn't imagined it. If she felt the same, that's all he needed to know.

He stood in front of her door, palms sweaty, heart pounding and breathing shallow. He shifted from foot to foot, took a deep breath then knocked. He hoped he wasn't being a fool.

Pain crushed his hopes a second later when the door opened and that dude stood on the other side. Tyrone took a half step back. The embarrassment and misery blowing through him robbed him of the ability to speak.

The guy had the audacity to smile. That made Tyrone's shoulders stiffen. If he was going to gloat, then Tyrone wasn't going to pretend as if he was here for anything other than to see Kiera.

"Hold up a second," the guy said. He looked over his shoulder. The sound of voices and laughter came from inside the apartment. "Hey!" he yelled and the laughter faded. "Kiera, your boy is here."

Tyrone frowned. So, this guy knew about him? There was a hush for a second before another male voice said, "Her boy?"

"He came! Terrence said he would," a strange female voice chimed in.

"Shut up!" Kiera said.

Two heartbeats later, she was shoving the guy aside and at the door. She'd changed out of the dress she had on earlier and was standing in front of him in loungewear and no makeup. She was absolutely beautiful. Then it hit him again. She was here, with that dude, with no makeup. Who the hell was this guy to make her feel that comfortable with him?

"Tyrone? Why are you here?" The sound of footsteps pounded behind her before a man and woman stood with the other guy.

He ignored the audience and focused on the look in Kiera's eyes. The longing there, the anticipation. Nah, he wasn't imagining that. "Um… I wanted to talk to you."

The woman behind her patted the shoulder of the guy Tyrone didn't recognize. "Oooh, he wants to talk."

Kiera scowled at them. "Will you sit down?" She turned back to Tyrone. "Um…let's talk." She came out into the hallway and closed the door behind her. From the sound of the scurrying on the other side, Tyrone was pretty sure her guests were listening at the door.

He pointed at the door. "Who's that?"

"My brother and his girlfriend."

"And…that other guy?"

She met his gaze. "My cousin Terrence. He agreed to be my plus-one for the party tonight."

Her cousin. Relief nearly buckled his knees. "Oh." He smiled so hard his cheeks hurt. She wasn't with someone else.

"Yeah, oh, is that the reason why you came by? To find out who he was."

"I did. I mean, you walked away with him."

She rolled her eyes. "Seriously, you only came over here to flex on my date?" She turned toward the door.

Tyrone reached out and placed a hand on her elbow. "No. Stop. Don't go back in."

She spun back toward him. "Okay, you came. You found out I'm not dating anyone else and what?"

"That's not the only reason. I mean, yeah, I got jealous when I saw you with him, but that's not why I went to that party. That's not why I went to five other Exploration Network parties. That's not why I never posted our agreed-upon statement about breaking up. I came here because it's been six months, I miss you. I love you. I don't know how to make some grand declaration, but all I know is that when we met, I didn't think my life would change, but it did. And I don't want to go back."

She sucked in a breath. "You—you love me. I…"

"Yeah, I love you, Kiera. I know when we started out, I asked you to be my fake girlfriend."

"Fake!" The muffled word came from the other side of her door.

Kiera kicked the door then waved a hand toward Tyrone. "Ignore that. Go on."

He'd never talked about his feelings like this with a woman. Much less in front of other people. A year ago, he wouldn't have made the effort. Today, as he looked at Kiera and realized there was no other woman he'd rather be with, he didn't care.

"I asked you to be my fake girlfriend and you were perfect. I fell in love with you. Your drive and determination. Your humor and humility. Having you in my life was a bright spot that hasn't lit up since you walked away. I didn't like it, but I understood why you walked away. I know it might take a while for you to completely trust me, but I'm willing to put in the work to prove that to you. I tried to give you space. I tried to give us both the time we needed to figure out if what we felt was real and for me it is. The last time I asked you to be my fake girlfriend. Today, if you think you can, will you please give me the chance to be your real boyfriend?"

She pulled her lower lip between her teeth. Her eyes widened and the emotion radiating back emboldened him. He took a step forward and placed his hand on her hip. Inside he rejoiced when she didn't pull away.

He stared into her eyes and prayed she saw the love and sincerity overflowing from his heart. "Can I be your boyfriend, Kiera? For however long you'll have me."

Her lip slid from between her teeth and she grinned. "You're lucky."

"Why?"

"Because I just happen to love you, too." She nodded and wrapped her arms around his neck. "Yes, Tyrone Livingston, you can be my boyfriend."

He grinned, lowered his head and kissed her. He wanted to kiss her forever but the door to her apartment opened. Her family clapped and cheered.

"It's about damn time y'all got back together! Can he come to family dinner now?" her brother asked.

Kiera laughed and continued to hold on to him. "I don't know. Do you want to come to family dinner?"

Tyrone pulled her tighter into his embrace. "Just try and keep me away."

* * * * *

For more fantastic fake dating romances, try these other Harlequin Special Edition books:

Falling for His Fake Girlfriend
By Shannon Stacey

A Soldier Under Her Tree
By Kathy Douglass

Available now!

COMING NEXT MONTH FROM

HARLEQUIN®

SPECIAL EDITION™

#2953 A FORTUNE'S WINDFALL
The Fortunes of Texas: Hitting the Jackpot • by Michelle Major
When Linc Maloney inherits a fortune, he throws caution to the wind and vows to live life like there's no tomorrow. His friend and former coworker Remi Reynolds thinks that Linc is out of control and tries to remind him that money can't buy happiness. She can't admit to herself that she's been feeling more than *like* for Linc for a long time but doesn't dare risk her heart on a man with a big-as-Texas fear of commitment...

#2954 HER BEST FRIEND'S BABY
Sierra's Web • by Tara Taylor Quinn
Child psychiatrist Megan Latimer would trust family attorney Daniel Tremaine with her life—but never her heart. Danny's far too attractive for any woman's good...until one night changes everything. As if crossing the line weren't cataclysmic enough, Megan and Danny just went from besties and colleagues to parents-to-be? As they work together to resolve a complex custody case, can they save a family and find their own happily-ever-after?

#2955 FALLING FOR HIS FAKE GIRLFRIEND
Sutton's Place • by Shannon Stacey
Over-the-top Molly Cyrs hardly seems a match for bookish Callan Avery. But when Molly suggests they pose as a couple to assuage Stonefield's anxiety about its new male librarian, his pretend paramour is all Callan can think about. Callan's looking for a family, though, and kids aren't in Molly's story. Unless he can convince Molly that she's not "too much"...and that to him, she's just enough!

#2956 THE BOOKSTORE'S SECRET
Home to Oak Hollow • by Makenna Lee
Aspiring pastry chef Nicole Evans is just waiting to hear about her dream job, and in the meantime, she goes to work in the café at the local bookstore. But that's before the recently widowed Nicole meets her temporary boss: her first crush, Liam Mendez! Will his simmering attraction to Nicole be just one more thing to hide...or the stuff of his bookstore's romance novels?

#2957 THEIR SWEET COASTAL REUNION
Sisters of Christmas Bay • by Kaylie Newell
When Kyla Beckett returns to Christmas Bay to help her foster mom, the last person she wants to run into is Ben Martinez. The small-town police chief just wants a second chance—to explain. But when Ben's little girl bonds with his longtime frenemy, he wonders if it might be the start of a friendship. Can the wounded single dad convince Kyla he's always wanted the best for her...then, now and forever?

#2958 A HERO AND HIS DOG
Small-Town Sweethearts • by Carrie Nichols
Former Special Forces soldier Mitch Sawicki's mission is simple: find the dog who survived the explosion that ended Mitch's military career. Vermont farmer Aurora Walsh thinks Mitch is the extra pair of hands she desperately needs. Her young daughter sees Mitch as a welcome addition to their family, whose newest member is the three-legged Sarge. Can another wounded warrior find a home with a pint-size princess and her irresistible mother?

YOU CAN FIND MORE INFORMATION ON UPCOMING HARLEQUIN TITLES, FREE EXCERPTS AND MORE AT HARLEQUIN.COM.

HSECNM1122

HARLEQUIN
PLUS

Announcing a **BRAND-NEW**
multimedia subscription service
for romance fans like you!

Read, Watch and Play.

Experience the easiest way to get
the romance content you crave.

Start your **FREE 7 DAY TRIAL** at
<u>www.harlequinplus.com/freetrial</u>.